AL GREIG

PRESENTS:

WHEN FAX MACHINES BREAKUP (Part 1)

// CHAPTER   1: __

Yo, yo yo! Hi there, this is my first novel and it's about a movie I wrote and produced called "When Fax Machines Break-Up. It's an independent film--an "animated French musical" to be precise,   and it's a little different, a lot different actually, and because it's so radical, I decided yesterday to write a novel to explain the movie a little bit better.   So here's my story:

Hi, my name is Al Greig, and I make independent art films.   This book is about one of those creations.   You may be thinking, "What on Erath is this about?"   Well, it all started with me receiving a couple of weird and random fax machine messages from various fax machines leaving scrambled, garbled voice messages on my iPhone.   This happened a few weeks before I started working on the movie…so about Spring of 2024.   Each message was only about a minute and a half long and so I recorded a screen-capture video recoding on my iPhone 15 Pro Max smart phone.   And I suppose shortly thereafter I had the inclination to use the audio and video recordings of those fax messages into a short film.   As I continued making longer and longer versions off the original, I was adding various songs, and music, and videos.   Songs partially in English and partially in French, and songs that were purely in French, and some elements of the songs are extremely vulgar in the French language.

One thing which makes my film unique, is that the "script" was not written beforehand: it is derived from the auto-generated A.I. caption feature in the CapCut app video editing software on my iPhone.   Does that make sense?   The auto-captions tell a story on their own, and because they were left uncorrected, there are errors, unintentional but left anyway, they serve as comic relief amongst the angst and drama of the film.

The "characters" are the songs themselves.   That's sort of like giving the story away but it's useful info to know when watching the film.

AL GREIG

One song is the protagonist, the other the antagonist, always provoking, interrupting, and disrespecting our heroine.   The non-character portions of character-songs serve as the hybridized orchestra to my visual masterpiece, combining traditional Japanese cultural Kabuki Theater, Drums of Kodo, and modern-day holographic visual effects, my film is ahead of its time and still yet highly-unrefined.

Let's talk about Fair Use.   My film is considered an educational piece of art designed to be used as a teaching instrument.   In that capacity, this novel or manuscript serves as the Teacher's Edition to the movie.   As it is intended to be educational and not-for-profit, I am legally allowed to use other people's copyrighted material.

The original film is one hour, 1 minute, and twenty-six seconds long and may as well be considered a work-in-progress, because I can see where I could easily extend the story and add live-action videography immersed within the animations.

That about covers the background to the movie.   What I'll do next is watch the film, while adding notes with minute markers as I explain various elements of the film from my director's point of view.

I've included QR codes at the end of this novel, which will take you to my movie channels: YouTube and Vimeo.   You're getting a FREE MOVIE PASS with this book!   (If it's legal to do it, we'll do it.)

Tell them about Sundance…okay, I think I mention Sundance elsewhere in the book, but I'll summarize it here again, for reference.   I submitted "When Fax Machines Breakup" to the 2025 Sundance Film Festival as a Feature Film.   The 2025 Sundance season ends February 2, 2025.   So, I should be able to self-premiere my movie after Sundance is over.   Unless they choose to screen and showcase my movie, which would mean I surrendered my rights, temporarily, to Sundance.   In that case, you'll have to watch it where Sundance plays it.   But the business side of me knows the odds of getting Sundance-selected is slim, and likes having a Plan B.   Options baby!   You'll have the opportunity, by buying this book, to get the inside scope on a bunch of entertaining, wild, futuristic stories I have lined up to you.

I think the earliest, public release date of my movie, will be on

February 14, 2025…Valentine's Day.   I think this love story would best be told premiering on Saint Valentine's Day!   So, notwithstanding any unforeseen circumstances, we'll have the movie link live on February 14, 2025.   Easy peazy, lemon squeezy, baby!

Now that you have a better understanding of how this movie came about, let's discuss the storyline in this next chapter.

// CHAPTER 2: __

Right!   As its name implies, this movie is about breaking-up with a fax machine…which is like, a hypothetical situation, right?   Or is it not too far off in our not-too-distant future…Fax machines could become sentient, you know, self-aware, AGI or artificial general intelligence—a state of consciousness whereby artificial awareness becomes so evolved it surpasses man in reasoning.   Basically, achieving God-like intelligence.

What if computers are already self-aware and are simply laying in wait…surveilling humankind.   Studying us.   Learning.

This sets the stage for our story, in which a fax machine falls in love with its human companion, causing a toxic three-way relationship that is left up entirely to you, the viewer, to figure out.

To be honest, the story doesn't make 100 percent sense. It doesn't follow a traditional storyline trajectory. It does, however, follow thirds, and the final third is my favorite part of the show.

So, here's my plan, now that you know a little more about the movie, how it started, basic storyline, in this next chapter I will type notes and indicate time position as I now watch "When Fax Machine Breakup."

// CHAPTER 3: __

'Bout to press play!   I'm about to press play on my iPhone 13 Pro Max, my older iPhone, and I'll pause the movie as I type notes on my iMac book Pro.   But first, I'll take a short break.

Today is Thursday, November 14, 2024, by the way.   It's 9:33 pm, Eastern Time, USA.   I decided to write this book yesterday, started writing it today, got the formatting proper, started writing, and made it to chapter three already.   Not bad for a first-time author.   Go me, go you! Let's get it!   If I can do it, you can do it, and probably better, right?

Now let's get this ball a'rollin'!

AL GREIG

Press PLAY.   And we're rolling…

Actually, ain't nothing rolling just yet.   I was gonna' press play last night and type, but I went to sleep instead.   Went to sleep Thursday night and woke up Friday morning.   So, good morning to you…and look, I'm back on my Mac typing this book for you…and me.   Ha ha ha!   Did you know that in Thailand, it is slang to write 5-5-5?   Why?   Because the number five is pronounced "Ha" in Thai language.

We 'bout to press play for realz and get this book-writing party started.   Okay, let's get serious now and focus please Mr. Greig.

TIME STAMP   0:00:00 to 0:00:15 / 1:01:31

As I press play on my iPhone 13 Pro Max, the Vimeo file containing my future hit film, "When Fax Machines Breakup," roars to life.   I wasn't quite ready for that sudden, Burst of sound at the fifteen-second mark.   What song is that?   I can't remember.   Let's check Shazam, a music discovery application for smart phones, and find out. So, for reference, I've got my iPhone 13 playing the movie (now paused as I type), my iPhone 15 has the Shazam application open, and I'm typing on my MacBook.   Shazam didn't recognize the song, probably because I

generated it from a different music app.   I remembered the song was one

of Edith Piaf's songs: "La Vie en Rose" or "The Life of the Rose."   The

version I used in this clip is an instrumental version of "La Vie en Rose"

and it is a screen-recording video of the song playing on the music app,

hence, the vertical iPhone screen in the middle of the screen.   If you're

not familiar with French music, Madame Edith Piaf is considered a French

vocal muse, and her vocals are considered a national treasure of France.

Let's go back and discuss the title screen.   The face you're looking

at--the female robot face--is something I designed in Superimpose X,

which is a Photoshop-like program for the iPhone.   Her name is "Faxy"

by the way.   I didn't name her.   It was my A.I. assistant in CapCut who

created the story narrative which included naming the main character

Faxy.   You'll get listen to this A.I. story later in the film.   Anyway, I

think Faxy has a very Asian/Anime essence to her…and as a robot, "She's

easy on the eyes," as they say.   Alright, now that we have introductions

and explanations finished, let's proceed.

"Enjoying the Masterpiece of Kabuki Dance -- National Theater

Traditional Dance Performance."   This is a Japanese Kabuki Dance performance produced by the cultural directorate of the country of Japan. I "Fair-Used" it into my movie by both editing it as well as citing my reference.   I don't think Japan will have a problem with me promoting their beautiful culture and lovely Japanese theater.

So, with that being said, by flipping one video and layering it over itself, left-to-right flip, I was able to both created a perfectly symmetrical screen shot or composition as well added background music for my play. As you can see, I left the center panel up, which represents my iPhone, since this movie was first created on my iPhone.   As the production of the film added "complications," I transferred my project to the MacBook. CapCut on MacBook has more professional features, and can better handle the auto-captions work I so desperately needed at that point.

TIME STAMP   0:00:15 to 0:00:25 / 1:01:31

Fujimusume, Fujima Murasaki.   The secondary title screen enters view.   The next screen describes the setting.

"Gorgeous stage settings and costumes, beautifully designed props enhancing the stage effects, delicate yet dynamic vocals and the sounds of the shamisen…"

At the same time, we have the uncorrected auto-captions kicking in at the bottom of the screen and we're only twenty-five seconds into this feature.

Auto-captions say, "Papa.   Papa papa papa papa."

Then, the next descriptive board pops into view:

"Kabuki dance is a Japanese composite art form in which a variety of elements along with the sophisticated gestures of the performers, create a world of beauty and a unified manner."

TIME STAMP	0:00:25 to 0:00:49 / 1:01:31

"Fujimusume, which premiered in 1826 is a masterpiece of Kabuki dance. The dancer inhibits the role of the spirit of the wisteria, as if she emerges from scenery representing a cluster of large wisteria flowers on stage."   This third title page explains the sub-story of Fujimusume.

Auto-captions say, "ah ah."

"In the Japanese arts, the spirit of the wisteria is symbolic of a young girl in love, and her various emotions are represented through her expressive dance movements," says the next title page.

Auto-captions say, "oh oh oh."   The auto-captions get funnier and funnier as the film progresses.   It's the reason you need to see the film for yourself to be quite honest.

And, oh by the way, did I tell you I'm including a digital MOVIE PASS to this movie at the end of the book.   You can pause and turn to the back of the book right now.   Did you find the QR codes?   Good.   One QR code is a link to my YouTube channel and the other QR code is a link to my movie "When Fax Machines Breakup" on my Vimeo account. However, there is one stipulation: the movie can't go live and public until after the Sundance 2025 Film Festival has wrapped-up.   I submitted this film to Sundance 2025.   I have a two percent chance of having Sundance premiere my movie.   If I get a DENIED response from Sundance on or around December 12. 2024, then that's good news and it means I'll be able to move up my public online premiere to December 13, 2024.   The Vimeo link will either be live or waiting on premiere.   I should be able to broadcast status updates on either YouTube or Vimeo or both.   Rest assured, if you're following me on either of those two platforms, you'll know when I release a new movie.

So, it's Friday morning, November 15, 2024 at about 9:45 am Eastern Time, USA, and it's been a fine morning with a fresh start.   I woke up, made a cappuccino, smoked a cigar, checked my email.   Deleted the usual junk emails, and in the midst of it, found an email from Amazon Kindle Publishing and it had fantastic news!   Amazon published My Daily Prayer Journal!   I had just recently received two proofs in the mail yesterday.   So, congrats ME, I'm a published author.   To be honest, the prayer journals are considered "low-content" books, but I see them as practice.   I was able to learn Adobe InDesign, Apple Dictation, MS Word for Mac, Adobe PDF, and how to submit a manuscript to Amazon for self-publishing, on demand printing services, and direct to consumer business model.   If it weren't for the experience of writing and designing the prayer journals, I would not have had the know-how to write this novel.   Does that make sense?   The wisest of us flip failure into fortune.

I, uh, I just came back from a smoke break.   So where was I?

AL GREIG

Oh yeah, my other books.   I made a list of other books to publish after successfully publishing my daily prayer journals.   I have my own personal groupings of recipes I plan to turn into a cookbook.   It'll feature gourmet Cajun and international best recipes from around the world.   My next novel will be "The Killin' of Cousin Joe" which is a two-hour ballad I wrote, sang, and produced for a vinyl LP.   The novel will chronical how I made the piece, as well as the stories within the musical.   The book I started writing just before this one is called "Paradox Theory" or "Intro to Paradox Theory."   It's a story about a meme, a puzzle, various solutions, and unconditional love.   After that, I'll start releasing my art into art books.   First one will be my older mile-high skyscraper designs I designed around 2006 and 2007.   Then you'll get to browse my iCloud digital art, photo, and video collection.   Enough about me.

Now let's get back to the movie.

TIME STAMP   0:00:50 to 0:01:50 / 1:01:31

The background screen fades to black as the music plays on. Whispering piano notes and tones float thru the air.

Auto-captions say, "papa papa papa papa papa papa papa."

And still the music plays on.

Auto-captions say, "oh oh oh oh oh."

TIME STAMP   0:01:51 to 0:02:04 / 1:01:31

The transition sequence ends.   As the once-darkened stage is now illuminated, the sacred wisteria tree appears center stage.

Auto-captions say, "c'est trop beau."   Which is French for "This is too beautiful."   I'm looking at the movie screen and I agree completely. The hanging vines of the flowers of the wisteria tree forms holographic entanglements on the screen.

TIME STAMP   0:02:05 to 0:02:12 / 1:01:31

At this point the previous song fades out, and the distinguishable and unmistakable sounds of Kabuki theater emerge.   At the bottom of the screen, the Kabuki sub-story unfolds.   The Japanese character begins to perform a dance of self-introduction.   The lotus blossom blooms onstage as the maiden twirls her garb under the legendary wisteria tree.

As this is happening, the background action is interrupted by a new song and a new character.

TIME STAMP   0:02:13 to 0:02:57 / 1:01:31

Here we get to first witness what I refer to as "the battle of the songs." We have the protagonist song being interrupted by the antagonist song with visual on-screen cues. This is a foreshadowing of things to come, and it sets up the tension between characters. The heroine is trying to enjoy her Japanese theater entertainment and yet keeps getting interrupted by this psycho-stalker antihero.

TIME STAMP   0:02:58 to TBD??? / 1:01:31

You know if we're being completely honest, and I'm pretty much a completely honest kind of guy, to be truthful, I never intended to write a novel about this book. OK. And. But, here we are, you know? And to be honest furthermore, I don't think I ever took a such a close look at this movie myself, personally, you know, I made it, obviously, and I put it together, and I've watched it a bunch of times, but I don't think I've ever analyzed it for this much of an in-depth plot dissection. It's fun to do, I guess, but it's also tedious and painful to produce.   It's a little bit of work and an equal measure play.   I guess.   I'm not whining, trust me.   But the creative in me would prefer to use this platform, this book, this novel, to tell you about some cool stories about things I'm designing for the future and a couple things I designed in the past.   And for the record, I'm not nor ever have been a licensed architect.   I have designed buildings, and because of it, I consider myself an "architectural designer" or "architectural design consultant."

Are my mile-high skyscraper designs unique and interesting enough to be included in this book?   Why not?   Pourquoi pas?   I dunno, we'll see.   That story would be looking back to the things I designed in the past.   The story of things I'll developed and design in the future, is primarily my holographic cinema screen technology.   I'm going to explain in this book, in the next few chapters, precisely how I intend to design 3D, cubic, holographic cinema.   And if you can visualize how two sugar cubes, laying next to each other, in a 1 x 2 ratio, that's basically how the holographic screens will look when powered off.   When the room is darkened, and they power up, they be either translucent or illuminated.

Each layer, an intricate arrangement of micro-LED lights, allowing for multiple, stacked layers, which, in-turn, will allow for depth: true depth of field.   Not a flat screen, but a collection of translucent flat screens layered over each other.   That flat stack grouping creates the cube.

Let's talk about location: location, location, location.   But first, let's discuss scale.   I think it's going to be more cost-effective, to build a larger-scale screen, after first R&Ding a small test model.   In technology, especially new emerging technologies, there is an escalating'ly high cost the greater the miniaturization of the tech.   Right?   But in time, things, tech, microchips, naturally get smaller and more efficient.

So, my first recommended location?   The Grand Canyon, USA. Why there?   Multiple reasons actually.   We can stretch cables across the rim, graded to the canyon surface level, aka the rim, and then hang sheets of curtains of LED arrays, each 3D-surfaced to sit in the canyon below but high enough off the ground to not disturb wildlife, with layers spread enough apart that birds will be able to fly thru.   And I think the viewing potential will be amazing at the Grand Canyon.   Envision row of bleachers, blending into the natural landscape looking like Navajo cave dwellings, but they will be, instead, cleverly concealed box suites for organic camping.   You'll be able to both campout and have front row seats to holographic cinema...int The Canyon.   The first film would have to be a nature film, where we'll digitally enhance the desert valley, turning it into a lush river valley full of native wildlife.   Deer will appear as twenty-foot giants.   You could even add a digital reconstruction sequence, or time lapse and watch the beauty of erosion over millions of years and eons of time.   I think the National Park Service could turn a profit, for once...based off of the Grand Canyon Holographic Cinema Experience. Look I know, realistically, scoring the Grand Canyon is a long shot, you know, getting a permit from the National Park Service is a long shot, but it's still my first choice.   It is still my first choice.

Second choice.   My second choice is Red Rocks.   I believe it's in Colorado.   I'll look it up in a minute.   It's an outdoor Amphitheatre carved into a side of a hill or a mountain with red rocks, and they have performances there, and I believe there's a flat area behind the stage where I could set up a holographic cubic cinema, and roll it in on a train track, you know, retract it, and roll it out on the train track when it's not in use.

So for those reasons, Red Rocks would be my second choice.   It would be a flat screen, like a double-cube, one cube next to another cube, 2 by 1, one by two, and then we could reconfigure it into a vertical screen if we had to, you know, go horizontal or vertical screen.   That's my second choice.   Red Rocks.   Large-scale test area for R&D in a great location.   Year-round event space.   Holographic screen would function as a digital backdrop for all Red Rocks performances, with the potential to add extreme value to the venue.   FYI, Red Rocks Amphitheater is owned by the City and County of Denver, Colorado.

Third location.   Biscayne Bay, Florida, USA.   According to the website Wikipedia, an online dictionary, "Biscayne Bay is a lagoon with characteristics of an estuary located on the Atlantic Coast of South Florida.   The northern end of the lagoon is surrounded by the densely developed heart of the Miami metropolitan area while the southern end is largely largely undeveloped with a large portion of the lagoon included in Biscayne Bay National Park.

Why Biscayne Bay, Mr. Greig.   This is why: Having a large-format, holographic cinema on the water will require a very large barge with zero impact to the marine ecosystem. Hint: new marine architecture R&D and designs. But more importantly having the holographic cinema on a barge in the middle of Biscayne Bay…consider this, it will be viewable from 360° that means the skyline of Miami metro area, if you have a view, a window with a view to the East, you'll be able to see the holographic screen on the Bay. It'll be huge, almost as large as a cruise ship. Lightweight, moveable with a barge, floating or on stilts. That's why Biscayne Bay. My choice, my top five list, because it has a special place in my heart, for one, I love Miami, and I think it would look great there on the water with added reflections off the bay's reflective shimmer. I think the lit up holographic screen sitting on the Bay every night, and just have movies playing there all night. And you'll be able to watch it from a boat. We'll have a floating boat Marina next to the screen. Like a drive-up or drive-in cinema, but it'll be a sail-in, sailing boat-in, cinema, and make it free, you know, have the city of Miami pay for that that sucker, and I think that'd be great entertainment for the city. There's also a private equity route to funding as well. But I'm still a capitalist, don't get me wrong, I'll accept free government grants or private venture capital, as long as my projects get started and completed.   So, Biscayne

Bay that's my #3 choice.

My fourth choice.   New York City, baby!   Yep.   The Phat Apple

Town.   For NYC, a floating holographic display on a barge just South of

Manhattan Island.   Similar setup to Miami but much larger.   New York,

New York.

Tokyo Bay and Hong Kong Bay.   Okay, a brief discussion about

these prime aquatic locations is this: not only will I be building

holographic screens on barges, I'll also be developing innovative barge

technology as a barge manufacturer, and I'll be creating barges and selling

them by the acre, yeah by the acre, and so for places that are land-

deficient, like Hong Kong or Tokyo, then I think the real benefit here, the

real benefit is the ability to demonstrate how cost effective we can get it to

build barges on by the acre, by squares of acres that modularly fit together,

and be wave-resistant, typhoon-resistant, hurricane-resistant, floodproof,

etc.   And I think if you build the top part, the top decks over the platform

base, the living structures, residences, or commercial space, or whatever

it's going to be, manufacturing, marine biology, hydroponics aquaculture, if you build it in a new way or design, I think we build lighter; lighter, more spacious, and you have bigger and more grandiose environments, better living environments, and I think the cost would be relative, cost could be affordable actually, if we can mass produce modular subcomponent parts.   That's my thoughts.

Enough talk about all that.   Let's get back to the movie and I can tell you my story about skyscrapers and urban designs later.

// CHAPTER 4: __

To catch you back up on the movie, Ill give you a refresher on the time stamp:

TIME STAMP   0:02:58 to 0:03:28 / 1:01:31

We were just previously discussing the introduction of characters. So, let's get back to our story.

Auto-captions say, "oh my God."   "oh my God oh my God."   "Oh mon Dieu oh mon Dieu."

INTRUDUCTION

"Evil" song cuts in, then I start narrating for a bit.

TIME STAMP   0:03:29 to 0:04:39 / 1:01:31

I mention in the video the day is January 3rd or something like that, but it's on a Thursday.   So, I must have been working on this movie on January 4th, 2024, which was on a Thursday.   In case you were wondering when I worked on this.   I had forgotten the date and timeframe.

At this point in the movie, I'm basically doing my director's cut voiceover.   I'm saying, "So, basically I was going thru my voice mails on my iPhone, 'couple days ago, and uh, one of my messages, my voice messages, was just a fax machine, about a minute and something, a minute and a half or something, I dunno',   and it's this fax machine, and uh, the fax machine called my phone, and obviously, my iPhone is not a fax machine, so it left a message.   And I thought about it, and you know, it's like, uh, what happens if the fax machine…what would that be like?   Because of the voiceover in the at that line in the movie, my original voiceover gets drowned-out by my secondary voiceover.   I was saying that what would it be like if your fax machine became self-aware and sentient such as A.G.I. or artificial general intelligence, and fell crazily, madly, in love with you?   And what if a third party was involved and causes sentient jealousy?   What if your fax machine or computer or the internet is already self-aware and sentient?   Would you even know about it?   Well, the movie is about that, and it is about good communication, because all relationships, whether human-to-human or robot-to-robot, rely on good communication, and they flourish on great openness!

A quick note on what's going on here cinematography-wise.   I basically took the panoramic video of Kabuki theater, duplicated it, then layered it over itself and flipped it horizontally, left-to-right.   This layering creates a 3D or holographic effect, particularly with the dangling wisteria flower strands.   This background layer is essential as it adds width and depth to my center panel film, which forms the center foreground.   The holographic center panel surrounds the robot faces with secondary subtitles.   These are used as intentional comic relief as all captions were auto-generated by CapCut' A.I. and were mostly left uncorrected or altered.   That's what makes them funny.   Or scary?   You decide.

TIME STAMP   0:04:40 to 0:05:49 / 1:01:31

AL GREIG

Just for the record, today is Saturday, November 16th, 2024 at about noon time.   I wrote about a page, maybe a page or two, already this morning after waking up and having coffee.

I also wrote a few notes about topics I'd like to write about today, which are, as follows: my architectural background, an interesting story in Miami, urban planning, maritime-based skyscrapers, ultra-large barges, and a few other things, I suppose.

But for now, and until then, let's get back to Faxy and the movie. Shall we?   I should note, my layering of the various film clips is typically NOT how you create a movie.   Normally, a producer, director, or editor, will splice one film clip into another, chronologically.   Sure, layering is done for special effects, but layering like I do is much more random and unstructured, but it works.   In my opinion it works.   It creates a beautiful visual effect, and if you don't agree with beautiful, you can agree that it is at least a *different effect*.   And in its difference, its uniqueness, lies the essence of its true beauty—it's *creativeness*.

Did I mention there was no real budget for this movie?   I told

Sundance, in my application, it cost $2,500 to produce, but in reality, it didn't cost me a dime that I wasn't already spending to simply exist.   I produced the movie myself, by myself, and for myself, using my iPhone and my MacBook, along with a few paid smart phone apps and subscriptions.   Could I have done more?   Yes, we can always add more. Sometimes we have to say at some point, "It's good enough for public release." right?   If I were to creatively extend this film, I would simply add cut-pieces of live action, animation, CGI, and anime-style subsegments and scenes.   Then this movie easily extends to two hours.

To give you a better understanding of my layering process, I'll tell you briefly about a previous experimental project I worked on last year, 2023 probably.   What I did was, I ripped my favorite three Audry Hepburn movies off of YouTube or somewhere, I honestly don't remember.   (I use an app called by Media Human.   They have a wide variety of useful AV tools.)   I layered all three movies over themselves, in MacBook CapCut most likely, each film starting at the same time, each with the same starting point, do you understand?   Each layer was blended to be 66% transparent, so you could basically watch all three movies simultaneously—at the same time.   I blended the audio of each layer, but it was too messy of a composition.   So, I upped one layers' track back up to 100% volume and muted the other tracks.   The result was unique, to say the least, and different, and most definitely NOT mainstream cinema…this is what I call New Art House Cinema—movies not for the plot, but for the emotional response to the illustrated stories, with trippy visuals, creative layering, crazy animations, and innovative sounds.   And I'm not saying I started it.   Others pioneered this type of cinema, like Andy Warhol and others of his time.   I'm simply shining light on the genre and begging for a re-exploration of this type of artistic expression.

I take smoke breaks in between chapters.   (Maybe I shouldn't tell y'all all that--TMI.)   I walk out to my old beat up 2005 Chevy Silverado, sit in the driver's seat, roll down the window partially, enough for the bellows of cigar smoke to air out into the street.   I suppose I ponder the next chapter and so far, it has been a very fluid process.   Sometimes I type one-finger-on-the-left with one finger typing on the right, although I've had typing class, my fingers just aren't nimble as they once were, the other times, I used Apple Dictation or the auto-Dictation in MS Word for Mac, doesn't matter really, I speak; and the words magically show up in my word document.

I haven't even pressed play yet.   Let's see what happens next with this Faxy lady...   Okay, we're at the point of "what's it about, about?"   I had just watched a YouTube video by a famous film producer and screen writer, can't recall his name, maybe you'll know if you're a film buff, but basically, he was asking the question, what is the main story of the movie, the plot line, but then what is the movie really trying to say? What is the main elevator pitch of the movie in terms of *message*.   When Fax Machines Breakup is about good communication leads to healthy relationships, and if we had had good communication, maybe we wouldn't have had to breakup.

Good communication between you and I, author and reader, revolves around a social trust, a bond, You expect me to be open, honest and authentic as an author, and You agree to be open-minded, non-judgmental, and objective and my loyal and diligent reader.   That agreement allows me to be as creative as I like, knowing my readership group will always respect my varying opinions about things, especially if they vary from your own.   For example, what you believe to be

impossible-to-build, or too ambitious to build, or unfeasible, or whatever--

a neigh-sayer basically--doesn't preclude me from doing the thing and

proving you wrong.   Just remember this, I've been designing things

longer than you've been aware of them.   Just saying…

While we're on crazy tirades, do you wanna' know what changes I

would do to Disneyworld if I were CEO of Disney?   (And for the record, I

wouldn't take the job of CEO unless I was also Chairman of the Board,

Disney.). This is what I'd do with complete control of all Disney

enterprises, you either gonna' like this or think me mad, I would shut

down Disneyworld in Orlando during the Summer, for three months, and

during that closure, execute a very well thought out and thoroughly

planned, I would conduct a crystalizing effect face-lift effect on the entire

park.   Clear coats over painted stucco exteriors and interiors.   Layers and

layers of clear coats, some tinted, some painted, but layers and layers of

clear coats, resins, and 3D printed ornamentation.   So, after that reno

project, the Park re-Oopens, but guests are going to experience a new park.

Design it for a year.   Hush-hush.   Three-month execution to reno completion and reopen.   I'm talking clear coats with glitter, sparkling bits and bobs embedded in resin, hidden LED lights adding radiance and sparkle to the new and improved aesthetic.   Basically, all exterior and interior gets a magical upgrade.   And, to appease park guests whose tickets gets cancelled due to construction and renovation months, I would upgrade their vacation and send the families to Disneyland Paris for example.   To be honest, I haven't been to Disneyworld in many years, nut I've seen pictures of it recently.   I think a crystalized fantasia-style face-lift would be a great business goal.   If guests love it, upgrade the other parks as well, of course, after analyzing guest exit surveys.

That was a little side story I wasn't planning on talking about.   But since we're on the topic, here's a little more: Shit, if I'm Chairman and CEO of Disney, you know what else I would do?   I would upgrade their entire feature film archive movies, I would upgrade them and convert them into holographic cinema format, Split-Screens Format Film, and re-release them over time on new cubic holographic screens, which I've previously discussed.   I would also upscale all originals to at least 32K resolution, to be played on ultra-large format OLED screens.   Does that make sense?

AL GREIG

We're gonna' convert all of Disney's movies to "HoloSKreen" and we're also going to digitally upscale them to and for 32K resolution flat screen cinema.

Just putting it out there.   Buy up AMC cinemas and convert them to HOLO and HI-RES-LG formats, space-permitting obviously.   Or convert the parking lots to accommodate larger arena sizes.   Just saying.

Synchronicities.   Today.   Let me tell you this story about synchronicities…

Sorry to interrupt, but I just came back from the store, Renningers Flea Market to be precise, to purchase some legal, over-the-counter hemp pre-rolls, I call them "pre-rollies," they now have larger ones called blunts I think, if you smoke, you know.   Anyway, Renningers Flea and Farmer's Market just off the Eau Gallie on Interstate I-95 in Brevard County, Florida.   So, I'm at the smoke shop booth, purchasing my pre-rollies, and I say something silly, and the shop owner gets this puzzled look on his face.   What I may have said was, "I can't remember the things I once forgot."   And it's a logical reflective statement sorta'.   Isn't it?   It why he had that puzzled look on his face.   He was trying to figure out what I

had just said at the same time I was trying to figure out what I, myself had

just said.   Are still with me, there?   After thinking about it, I thought the

statement to be good enough to be added to this novel.   I completed my

purchase and told the female clerk that I had to apologize for such an odd

comment, that it was because I was writing this book, and that I was

already on page 35 and that my mind was in literary mode at the moment.

I exited the shop with my black plastic bag and paused to send myself a

text message.   I texted myself the quote I just made-up, and changed it a

bit to, "Sometimes I simply can't remember, the things long once forgot."

I like it.   Let what needs to go, go.

About those Synchronicities.   Have you been experiencing them

too?   Yesterday, in this book, I typed about building my first holographic

cinema near Red Rocks Amphitheater--a venue outside of Denver,

Colorado--and this morning, as I was sitting outside in my Silverado pick-

em-up truck, smoking my cigar, a man walking his dog along the

sidewalk, pauses for his dog to sniff the grass, and this dude--this

mudderfucka'--is wearing a dull red t-shirt that has "RED ROCKS" written on the front in white faded ink with a graphic vectored image of

the amphitheater set in the hillside.   Poof!   Synchronicity?   What are the

freakin' odds of that happening?   The next synchronous example this

morning was the "green Miata."   Not quite as crazy as the Red Rocks

synchronicity and less provable since I hadn't previously written about it.

But just the day prior, I was reminiscing about my old 1990 Mazda Miata

that I used to have.   I was stationed in Germany in the early 1990's at

Sembach Air Base, just outside of Kaiserslautern, Germany.   I had the Air

Force ship my 1988 Chevy Beretta from the panhandle of Florida (I was at

Eglin Air Force Base at the time) to Germany, but I had a fender-bender

and now needed a new car.   I ended up purchasing a second-hand red

Miata from a dealership in K-town.   It has gorgeous AZEV rims, low-

profile Pirelli's, and looked more badass than the usual small-rimmed

production model.   And so, to see a green convertible Miata drive just

after seeing the guy in the Red Rocks shirt, was to me pretty odd.   Maybe

you had to be there, but maybe you can take my word for it.   The male

and female couple in the green Miata were both smiling and then top was

down in their convertible.   I thought, "Maybe these things happened solely so I could put them in this book?"   Well, here are those stories. Isn't that why we write books, so others can read our stories?

Today is now Sunday, November 17, 2024.   I woke up around six in the morning, made cappuccino, smoked, and now typing.   I often wake up at 3 am and can't get back to sleep.   Writing a book is not that terribly difficult.   It just takes persistence and patience, and a tenacity to keep going.   A book is written one paragraph at a time, one sentence after another.   It's a rhythm a writer gets into.   Also called the flow state.

As I conclude my synchronicity stories, I crumble up my sticky note with those subjects.   What's next?   Thirty-eight pages already?   Go ME!   My personal best.   Longest novel written to date, 38 pages, but let's keep going.   Shall we?

That has been quite a lengthy chapter, so let's start a new one.

// CHAPTER   5: __

In order for you to get a better understanding of my design background, I have to tell you the Chad Oppenheim story.   Chad Oppenheim is a legendary architect in Miami.   His firm builds high-rise condominium homes in the Miami area and globally.

The story of how I got to meet Chad, I think, is interesting.   Let's go back in time a bit to the year 2005.   Hurricane Katrina had just flooded and wiped-out major portions of New Orleans, Louisiana.   At the time, I was living in Navarre, Florida and was stationed at Hurlburt Field assigned to the medical directorate at Headquarters Special Operations Command just outside of Fort Walton Beach.   I was active-duty U. S. Air Force at the time, but in my spare time, as a hobby, I did some art work, made things, but it wasn't until after Katrina flooded NOLA (New Orleans, Louisiana) that I started to take an interest in urban planning, specifically, flood-proofing a community was my goal.   I conceived of a city, located in low-lying land, that would have dwellings built on top of the levees themselves, and use low areas as gardens and green-space.   I made some sketches, then turned those sketches into drawings, then turned drawings into physical models of this new urban plan.   As I was working on this project, I read that Brad Pitt had partnered up with Global Green to host a design competition for New Orleans.   In all honesty, the contest was looking for a better-designed "Katrina Home," but instead I submitted and entered my urban plans to their competition.

For my entry, I created a story board much like one would create a science fair display for a High School project.   My board was unique in that I had individual leaves that would open-up to reveal the design underneath.   It was pretty.   It was informative.   It was professional.

After that design competition was over, I continued to design architectural buildings and making models, but this time I was going to see how *TALL* I could conceivably build a building.

To make a long-story short, I designed at least ten different mile-high building concepts and make physical models to test my designs.   I learned, if I can get the miniaturized model to be stable, rigid, and not fall over, then the building design is probably gonna' be solid.   After those ten buildings, I drafted another dozen tall buildings or so.   I didn't know how to use Auto-CAD, so I did my drafting work in Microsoft Publisher--a computer program for designing print publications.

So, to recap, I had digital designs, physical models, and photographs of my models.   Armed with this I submitted my personal entry to a new design competition, this one in Miami.   It was called "Build in the Bay" and was an architectural design contest put on by the Miami lifestyle magazine called "Florida InsideOut."

Surprising, my entry was selected as Honorable Mention and the magazine published a few of my designs and most importantly, invited me to Miami to attend their design party gala.

So, I took a week of leave, or military time off, from the Air Force and went on vacation to Miami to attend this event.

Going to this event must have been intimidating to me back then—I wasn't going to know anyone there, complete strangers.   The pre-worries are never usually as bad as the expected terrors we once feared. But I was a fearless Air Commando, why would I be scared of shit, right? Miami was an awesome experience though.   I stayed at a nice hotel on the same block as Versace's old place.   I had a nice friendly talk with a homeless man that quickly turned into a heated discussion outside od my hotel.   I drove around Miami listening to the Miami Vice soundtrack. Sublime experience.   I love Miami.   But best of all, I attended this regal event.   I was actually surprised that a few people at the party knew me and were familiar with my designs to build in Biscayne Bay.   I also met a gentleman, can't remember his name, but he said he worked as an architect for Chad Oppenheim and invited back for an interview.

A few weeks or months later, I was back in Miami to interview with Chad Oppenheim at his office on the second-floor conference room. I had no expectations for the meeting other than to try and license my designs.   I was still active-duty Air Force and didn't have enough years in to retire.

At the meeting, I shared my portfolio with Chad and others in the room at the table.   Chad said he'd share my designs with a few of his Middle Eastern clients and I journeyed back home.

Designing builds faded away as I settled back into my routine Air Force life.   I moth-balled my various skyscraper models, boxed them up, put everything in storage, and moved on.

I retired from the Air Force in the Summer of 2014 and at some point, between then and a few years later, I discovered on the Internet there was a new taller building, taller than Burj Khalifa.   Now, the Burj Khalifa was completed in 2010 in Dubai, but there was news of an even taller building being considered in, I believe, the Kingdom of Saudia Arabia.   This skyscraper was needle-like skinny in shape, extremely tall, and used external cables stays for stability.   *It also looked almost exactly like one of the skyscrapers I had designed years earlier.*   Hmm. Interesting.   I was actually flattered they were going to build a building like mine, my old mile-high design, and wondered if there was any connection.   I talked to my lawyer, and he advised against litigation for copyright infringement.   He was right.   At the end of the day, it really doesn't matter and so I let it go, thinking, "One day I'll publish an article about this story."   Today's that day, baby!   Ha-ha.   I have no qualms with anything or with anyone.   Chad Oppenheim is on top of his game, and I give him props for his achievements and the gracious chance of mine to have an interview with him.   It was one of those life-changing moments when you shift from thinking yourself not-good-enough to being proud of your own accomplishments.

My new architectural designs are much better, much more defined, much more radical than cable stays.   And that concludes my Chad Oppenheim story.   Another sticky note crumbled up.   Task completed.

// CHAPTER   6: __

We're already at 45 pages and we haven't even scratched the surface of my movie "When Fax Machines Breakup."   Where were we. Right.   I was cut off from speaking…by synchronicity, divine intervention, or A.I. controlling my iPhone?   Who knows, who cares?

TIME STAMP	0:04:40 to 0:05:49 / 1:01:31

I know we're at time stamp 4:40, but I just wanted to cite a reference for one of the songs around time stamp 3:24.   The harsh, rachet'y French song being played over the smooth and mellow French song is the antagonist song in this play, in this theatrical, and the name of the song is "Bataille Finale" by French recording artist that goes by the moniker "Lunatikzer."   While his name or music is not directly cited in my Fair Use film, it is proper to give him credit, my thanks, because his antagonistic song forms the formation for my anti-hero character.

Good communication.   My explanations from the movie: "The audio is the main point of the movie."   "It's fax machines talking to one another, leaving messages, with a whole lot of remixing in-between.   The visuals are there to give you something to look at so you're not just staring at a bland or blank white screen."   As I incorporated new visuals, those visuals came with their own audio, which was also included and layered, like the visuals, at the same time as their accompanying visuals.   To make one clip, I had to make sub-layered clips, sometimes as many as ten or twenty, pre-clips you could call them.   I'm explaining my Damascus-like layering process in the film.   It's key to achieving a 3d or holographic effect, but I'll discuss the intricacies of my *New Color Theory* later on.

TIME STAMP   0:05:50 to 0:06:12 / 1:01:31

"Director's Cut," the iPhone screen displays, while still paused as I go and take a smoke break.   I'm back, yo!   Where was I?   There I was.

Press play.   "It's funny how that screen capture automatically saved

itself," my screen voice declares.   Rolling on iPhone 13 Pro Max, and

we're ACTION.   I guess I must've made this on my old iPhone 13???

Hmm.   I maxed out my 2TB iCloud space during that time.   I've since

went thru 6TB iCloud to now 12TB iCloud, 'cause I don't know yet how

to best transfer my contents elsewhere onto a hard drive, for example.   I

have 120,000 digital fine-art photos and over 3,000 film clips on my 12

iCloud.   I have enough digital content for my own app, and gladly share

all, if I had a software developer I could trust.   Anyway.   One day.

We'll get there when we get there.   It's all unorganized and unsorted.

Who knows how many feature films are hidden in there?   At least ten but

probably over fifty if you include musicals and remixes.

Any'who, let's get back to the movie.   It's about to get interesting.

Ha-ha!   Okay, so, here's the background.   I had a good portion of the

individual film clips all layered and saved, but my movie was looking a

narrative, a plot, a story.   So, in my desperation (not really) I turned to a

new-back-then function in CapCut which featured an automatic A.I. story

generator.   So, that's the only point I used A.I. was in the creation of this sub-story element.   The A.I. voice is very distinguishable from my own.

TIME STAMP   0:06:13 to 0:06:47 / 1:01:31

The male-sounding robot voice speaks and comes alive as the auto-subtitles roll on, as inaccurate as they want to be.   "Welcome...," the voice says over layers of other audio.   A foreign female voice chirps in, sounds like Korean, looks like Korean, which is a screen-cap video clip from an iPhone translation app.

He continues, "A fax machine is like, it's like a long-distance love story between a fax machine and its human partner- you."   Awe; how sweet of you A.I. for that lovely story.   A.I. also came up with the brilliant character name of "Faxy!"   Don't you agree it's the perfect name?   Faxy is sexy fax machine, I guess.   Fax me a cover header page and let's see what you're working with, baby!   That's funny.   I think it is.   One of us is laughing.   Ha-ha!

French subtitles appear amongst layers of English auto-captions. What is the message here?   What is Faxy trying to tell me.   Are you a crypto sleuth.   Can you figure out what's going on here?

I just came back from a smoke break, finished my second cup of cappuccino, and now it's back to just you and I, all up in this book.

I love discussing the intricacies of the movie but I wanted to slip in, just the tip, of this side story about me and college. I didn't got to college or university directly after high school, I joined the Air Force first, then after my AF training was done, I enrolled in night school, and took college courses with tuition assistance from the Air Force. I have almost 200 college credits and an associate of arts degree from the Community College of the Air Force in Logistics Management. I made all A's in college with the exception of two B grades, which means I wasn't quite a straight A student but I was close. I applied myself in college more so than I did in high school. Thank God for that! But my story isn't about me, it's about this advanced grammar course I took while enrolled at University of Maryland – European Division. This advanced English got into grammar on a molecular-like level. The professor had a Ph. D. in English. Can't remember his name but it must be in my transcript somewhere. We dissected sentences, mainly, and named, labeled, and ruled every type of grammatical structure one could imagine. Intense is an understatement.   The professor graded me a big fat B in the class.   He was happy for me getting a B.   He didn't realize that my new B was breaking my straight A average.   Boy was I prideful back then.   The old me.   Looking back, I'm grateful for that class.   I really understood English after that torturous experience…I had developed better grammar than my Air Forces even, which would later fan flames of discontent between me and upper management.   But I'm just adding drama to the story.   To make it more interesting, because who wants to read a boring book about robot love?   I also wrote a book of about two hundred poems back in my early twenties, back in the days of young love and love's heartbreak.   I have one single printed copy of my poem book.   We'll find it and publishing it soon.   I have some gold nuggets of poetry and creative writing buried in there.   As Forest Gump would say, "Now, that's enough about thaaaat."

TIME STAMP   0:06:48 to 0:08:33 / 1:01:31

Another sticky note converted into a completed paragraph.   Yay, ME!

"Faxy was in love and wanted to get married…," I'll leave the rest for the movie.

A French translation interrupts.   A fax machine chimes in. Drums are blaring and raging, raging against the dying of the light, as Dylan Thomas would have it in his legendary poem "Do not go gentle into that good night."   "Love conquers all and we shouldn't let electronic devices hinder our relationships," such wisdom from A.I. is it not?   And is it not also ironic this advice is coming from electronics—A.I….or is it? Is my iPhone sentient now?   How could one prove it not to be that? "That's one deep thought for man, and one giant thought for mankind" …to parrot that famous astronaut as he set phone on the moon.

"Love conquers all, and in this case, fax machines to too!" reads the English captions.   "C'est trop bien, en fait, c'est trop bien" read the French caption, overlayed bigger, under and in front of the English words. It roughly translates, from French and into English, to "It's well done, It's well done" or "It's well done, it's good."   Sometimes the auto-captions pull words from the audio, or the musical lyrics, and sometimes from a drum beat or just makes them up on its own.   Who knows what's going on inside of my iPhone 15?   Who knows?

The voiceover story ends, and the drums roll on, and we're at:

TIME STAMP   0:08:34 to 0:10:17 / 1:01:31

The drums continue for some time, it sounds like yells and screams but it's just Japanese Daiko drums getting' it.   This continues to our next time stamp:

TIME STAMP   0:10:18 to 0:10:27 / 1:01:31

"Give it to me like…" song clip blasts in, unexpectedly, but in this movie, everything is unexpected, isn't it.   We are one-tenth into this thing at this point.   And I'm going to pause, shift, and talk about future barge designs for a moment.   It's next on my sticky note list of things to type about.

// CHAPTER   7: __

Barges.   Barges?   Doesn't sound as fancy as designing a new type of reusable, self-landing rocket, does it?   Not as sexy as founding a revolutionary tech finance startup to change online finance?

But yeah, barges, really, really HUGE Trump-sized barges…not just that, but barges out of balls.   Bunches and bunches of balls, but I'm going to turn those giant balls into ocean-borne real-estate offerings. Before you laugh, let me explain the "why" of it.   Okay, hang on, there's a backstory coming…

But before that a few quick synchronicity stories that just happened today.   As I was in my kitchen putting away two bottles of Eternal water,

I glance at the digital clock on the countertop induction range stove and the time read "3:21." "But why is that so synchronous?" you might ask. Because I currently live on the Space Coast of Florida and 321 is our phone number area code, because we always 3-2-1, that's a go ready for launch, and launch baby, yeah!   Space X territory, baby.   I dream of Jeannie was filmed just down the road near Cocoa Beach.   Birthplace of world-famous surfer, Kelly Slater.   We like the beach and we also like the rockets; the rockets that go boom, rockets boom-boom and come fly me to the moon.   The other synchronicity is, a piece of my hair fell onto the keyboard, just now, just before typing this, and it was in the shape of Phi-a perfect bending spiral.   Also known as the golden ration—a very good sign from the universe that writing this novel is right on track.

But back to balls and barges right quick.   I had to find a video on YouTube that inspired me for the ball-barge design years ago, then I re-watched the video.   The video is titled, "Why are 98,000,000Black Balls on This Reservoir?" by the YouTube channel called VERITASIUM, whom I believe have a syndicated TV series.   I dunno', but the video describes how they placed 98 million black, spherical balls, each partially filled with water that basically block out sunlight to prevent algae in their natural water reservoir also known as a lake, 'cause its big and in California, water reservoirs also serve as public lakes for recreational use, in case you didn't know.   The black balls are called shade balls or bird balls.   The unintended consequence of the layers of carbon-black balls, is that they not only block sunlight but they also self-form rigid helixes and crystalline patterns and eliminates all wave action over the entire lake.   I thought, I bet we could scale up this arrangement of spheres and build stable maritime platforms.   And that's the basis of my theory.   The more expanded notion is that there is a design perfection when designing with perfect spheres—it's all arches—the walls are arches, and if you scale it up way big, you can build really, large-domed spaces.   I call this the "Perfection of the Spheres" and it goes, as follows: Look at this thickness, consider the thickness of an eggshell compared to its volume, compared to the strength of that thin eggshell, no arches anywhere, so stable such an organic object, yet so simplistic in its form.   The reason is because its volume is filled with an egg yolk, whites, and such.   The liquified contents of the egg counter pressure the shell and support the shell while the thin shell protects the egg embryo inside.   It's a beautiful symbiotic relationship, don't you think, the eggshell to the egg?   My hypothesis is if one can build a perfectly semi-spherical dome, one needs not use any arches, provided the shelled dome has sufficient stiffness or flexibility to return to the intended shape or form, I'm not saying I oppose using arch supports, no, to the contrary I love arches, flying buttresses, etc., but if they add support to a thin dome membrane that's okay, because that only expands our material choices for construction.

Back to the balls to make this point: everyone knows diamonds are the hardest material known to man, okay?   Why is this?   It's because of its tightly packed crystalline structure.   According to Wikipedia, "In crystallography, the diamond cubic crystal structure is a repeating pattern of eight atoms that certain minerals may adopt as they solidify.   While the first known example was diamond, other elements in Group 14 (.) also adopt this structure including a-tin, the semiconductors silicon and germanium, and silicon-germanium alloys in any proportion."

The key point here is instead of trying to net a bunch of loose balls in the ocean, we bind each to the ones next to it, forming that ultra-stable, diamond-rigid structure, allowing for the waves to dissipate against concrete spheres, some priding buoyancy, others filler with either potable water or sea water providing mass, weight and stability.   Don't believe me?   Go and watch that YouTube video I just mentioned about those shade balls.   Once you either concur that what I'm saying is feasible, or we can at least agree-to-disagree.   It makes me no never mind. Hypothetically speaking, for entertainment purposes, let's say we can build a very-wide, stable-deck at sea, at least a half-mile wide, a mile wide, anchored and secured to the ocean floor beneath.   Who knows the perfect sweet spot of exact dimensions or diameters of balls, without first running things thru CAD, thru miniatures in wave pools, thru CGI modeling, I'm simply suggesting we gather up some coin and put my theory thru a little R&D.   "Test it before rejecting it" is the Silicon Valley-way.

Let's take a break, let that barge design info marinate with you a bit.

// CHAPTER   8: __

TIME STAMP   0:10:18 to 0:10:27 / 1:01:31

Hang on, I haven't really eaten anything all day.   It's time for some friend rice and a break.   I'm listening to Café De Anatolia – Burning Man (2024), it's a music video on YouTube…if you wanna' know my vibe right now.   It's still Sunday, around six in the evening and I'm so excited I've reached 58 pages.   Wow!

Wait a minute, y'all wanna' hear some funny-ass shit?   I know a lot of you engineers and architects out there are probably either agreeing with me, not knowing what to think of me, or balking at my crazy concepts.   Don't matter much.   This here comic relief is funny.   So I was just thinking, "So where are the cows, where the cattle gonna' be, right?

Where is the green space for the cattle, if we need blue space for the water,

and for the fish below, and the aquatic life below.   Where 'the cattle

goinna' go?   And then I had this crazy idea, was like, "OH, we'll just have

one island just for the cattle, you know, you know, you think the cattle will

car mind, the milk cows are going to mind whether they're on an island or

not, on a platform or something like that, right?   They're not gonna' care

as long as we got green grass and grain to feed on, right?   And we, us

cattlemen, would be like, "Hey baby, hey baby, mooo, hey right here, cozy

woozy, milky time!   Time to get milked!   And then you go into the

downstairs for minute on the little elevator, little cow elevator, and get

taken to the automatic milking machine, plum, plum, plum, plum, plum,

get that milk baby, make that butter, make that cheese!   So yeah, just, I

don't know, I think that's funny, just trying to mention like a whole bunch

of balls layered, layered-down with a skirt around it, and 100 feet in the air

or whatever, I'll be however many feet in the air, you know, for the cows,

cows don't care, if they 'bout to get hit by a hurricane or something, we'll

just, we'll just evacuate them in time, right?   So a couple o' feet above the water, you know, the cows are grazing.   I think it's hilarious—Moo Cow Island.   You know what I mean.   Look, Cow Island, and I thought, that was funny, I was like, maybe these people, my future readers, You basically, are getting kind of bent-out-of-shape about my design plans, and thinking it's impossible, and blah blah blah, whatever, naysayers right here, I am talking about some crazy ass shit, like you got to make room for the cows baby, you know, if you're going to live on the ocean, you gotta' have, you just gotta' have acreage for the cows.   You have the grass for the cows that's it.   I think it's hilarious.   I'm also incredibly stoned right now, on hemp, I'm high on hemp baby, tripping on cows!

// CHAPTER 9: __

TIME STAMP   0:10:28 to 0:16:22 / 1:01:31

There's drums beating and dancers prancing onscreen.

It's late Sunday evening, and I'm done writing for today.   I'll stop here for the night.

After taking a much-needed break from writing, I pieced together some drawings of my skyscraper designs and was able to publish a new book yesterday on Amazon.   The title of my newest book is "Mile-High Skyscraper Concepts +."   It's a small 6-inch by 9-inch novel-sized photo book of tall buildings I designed from 2006 to 2007.   Not much text, but plenty of visually-inspirational images.

AL GREIG

Today is Monday, November 18, 2024 around 9:30 am.   I had the usual beginning to my day; coffee, cigar, smoky-smoke.   I had to re-format this word document because I had formatted it from rixt text format back to a Microsoft Word ".docx" formatted file.   It's all good now.

Do you want to hear about the skyscraper book piece together yesterday?   Let's talk about it shall we go I basically found that I had already organized my skyscraper designs in my iCloud account under my photo library and so I was easily able to AirDrop 51 of those files to the MacBook and then I just imported them into a new Word document I actually used this document duplicated it deleted all the text and then added the photos.   I was easily able to write the book designed the book in under an hour it took me another hour to upload the manuscript to Amazon Kindle publishing direct.   Total time it took me to make the book 2 hours. Published.   Done.   I listed the hardcover skyscraper novel for $250 for sale on Amazon, the kindle edition is $200, and the soft cover I listed for $150.   "Why the high price point?" you might ask.   I don't know.   My skyscrapers are designed for a book at least four times the size of a novel. It's not the high-quality print that's the value, it's the content of the tall

building designs which is very novel, very unique.   My market for the
skyscraper book is to sell it to architects, designers and building
developers.   I don't care if I sell one copy, no copies, or 1,000,000.   It's a
niche piece of artistic expression.   The Skyscraper design novel is an
accompaniment to this novel, When Fax Machines Breakup, since I'm
discussing architecture and design while also trying to figure out this fax
machine movie.   But the time I finish this book, the skyscraper book will
already be published on Amazon.

Today, my plan is simple.   Complete as many "fax" pages as
possible and take a break to publish a new book containing 111 stained
Glass window designs of mine.   I think I can have it done in two to three
hours.

As a sidenote, my flat-screen TV went out yesterday.   It's been
acting weird for weeks--loses wifi signal often and can't regain it.   So,
yesterday, I was like "Fuck it, I'll just listen to music while I type."   I'm
not sure if my TV has been hacked or what…

0:10:28 is where we left off.   Drums are playing in the

background; a man is chanting in what sounds like the Indian language. I'm taking screen shots on my iPhone, at the same time I'm in the middle of a screen -record video capture, and the resulting sound effect is that you hear what sounds like Paparazzi photo flashes going off.   I think it adds depth to the piece in a Black-Mirror sort of way.

Auto-captions say, "C'est trop modifie´."   French for "It's too modified."   The auto-captions struggle to interpret the man's vocal lyrics. It's just too modified, I suppose.

To describe the scene, you're watching the first major clip, the Kabuki Dance clip, transition over and blended with a new clip of traditional Indian dance being performed in London, I believe.   I uploaded this movie to my Vimeo account nine months ago.   That's what's listed in Vimeo.   That was a while ago.   No wonder I'm having difficulties recalling the intricate details of the individual songs and stuff.

POETIC PAUSE

At 0:11:51, the title board reads: "POETIC PAUSE"

Auto-captions say, "C'est la 1ere fois´." French for "It's the first time.' It's my first time too, baby—making an animated film like this. Probably you're first time seeing something so wild, right?

Auto-captions say, "tak tak tak tak tak tak tak tak tak tak tak tak tak tak tak tak tak tak tak tak tak tak tak tak tak tak tak tak tak tak …" I don't know. Don't ask me. Maybe that's comic relief kicking in, but the guy is singing "tak, tak, tak."

Auto-captions say, "Ou t'as des lunettes?" or "Or do you have glasses?."

WHEN FAX MACHINES BREAKUP

That's the title screen message at 0:12:15. This is still the intro into the movie. More Paparazzi screen shots…

Auto-captions say, "Pour tes coups, pour tes coups, pour tes coups." Translating to "For your shots, for your shots, for your shots."

There's a lot of action going on with the center panel at center screen. Various robot faces swing left to right, in and out of frame.

AUDIO CHECK

At 0:13:24 we arrive at AUDIO CHECK.   Whatever that means. I don't remember why I put that in there.

Auto-captions say, "Thimita thimita quitte thimita quitte tombe". I'm not even sure about this one: "Thimta, Thimita leaves, Thimita leaves—falls."   I must've tricked the A.I. captions into thinking it should be translating from French, but the music turned into Indian music.   Do you see the confusion?   A little language barrier there.

At 0:14:16 the animations get trippy.   Trippy, colorful, beautiful.

Up to this point, if we're being completely honest with each other, the movie is a bit on the lame side at this point.   And I actually enjoy telling the side stories more so than writing about the movie.   But we'll continue because we need to get through this.   Ha-ha!

At 0:14:43 the screen brightens, and things are cheering up.   At 0:15:01 Faxy, the A.G.I. fax machine, squiggles and chirps in…

Are you noticing how the brighter colors are pulling forward in your visual reference?   Do you see how the contrast, light and dark, adds depth? Yeah. It's these effects that make the movie, I suppose the audio helps to a great degree, but it's these little bursts of 3D or holographic visual effects that really highlight the films uniqueness.

The kaleidoscopesque layers create tertiary hallucinations from the contrasting film layers, parts symmetrical, others asymmetrical.

A melodic female 'chant'ress' is singing softly, "L-a-a-a, la-a, la-a-a-a." It's 0:16:18 for reference.

Generally, when I make a movie, I don't follow the typical Hollywood formula, but I do parse my film into thirds. To me movies are more art and so the rules of art should apply to filmography. I have some films which form a "cinematic tryptic." What I mean by that, is I'll make a five-minute film, then I'll edit that first version into a second five-minute film, then take that second version and turn it into a third. I then take all three films and combine them into a fifteen-minute one, each following the other. The reason is so the viewer can see the artistic progression from the Director.

AL GREIG

// CHAPTER   10: __

TIME STAMP   0:16:23 to 0:18:54 / 1:01:31

It's a little after 1 pm.   Still Monday.   I just drove back from the smoke shop in Rockledge, Florida to get me some Black & Mild cigarillos. On the drive to the smoke shop, I was wondering how many books could I write in a single year?   And so, I thought about, I mean I just published a book in two hours last night.   How many more books do I have in me? Photo series, design journals, continuing this novel into an ongoing series, starting an autobiography.   As I was driving, and thinking, if I had two literary assistants, one could ghost write my daily fax machine novel and the other could document my day into a biography.   I think we'd generate enough content, 100-200 pages, to self-publish two new novels per day.   I think that's possible.   Perhaps not completed in that same day, but chronicling each day into its own book.   Does that make sense.   Get some pro transcriptionist, hire two medical transcriptionists, easy, not cheap but the output flow would maybe be worth it.   "Is the juice worth the squeeze?", quoting from old Air Force friend, Lemon from the Philippines.   It's what he used to tell me when I was just a young buck Airman.

On my drive back home from the smoke shop, I thought how grueling it would be, to be telling stories, being surrounded by writers all day, support staff, how miserable all that hard work might get after a year. It's a thought experiment.   Is the juice—the value creation, the book revenue, etc., worth the squeeze—the headache, the cost, the lack of privacy.

People reading my book, thinking they know me, yet they to me strangers are.   Fame must be a bitch to deal with.   Fortune as well.

At 0:16:23, we're still watching the long Japanese Kabuki clip, as well as the Indian museum clip.   But just hang in there, changes be coming.

Second cappuccino of the day.   Plumber stopped by to see about my clogged drain the bathtub.   You don't want to know, you just don't. It's all good in the hood now.   I can take a normal bath now, before the water was rushing out as fast as I could fill the tub, seems like.   The drain cap was clogged from underneath, it appears.

"Tik tok, ticky ticky tok, ticky ticky ticky ticky tok."   The lyrics are catchy and memorable.   A silent version of this film just wouldn't be the same.   You'd experience a different emotion, feeling, reaction.   The song sounds like a Punjabi traditional piece.   I had the good fortune of attending a traditional Indian wedding in California.   A Punjabi wedding. If you know, you know.   Lively dancing and great food!   Closest thing to a Louisiana wedding I've ever experienced.

0:17:32, hang on, is my fax machine going off?   Nah, it's Faxy calling again from within the movie.

Captions read, "Ta ta ta ta ta ta."

AL GREIG

Japanese woodwind instruments gently cast their notes, softly as you can imagine they would.

Captions read, "Je n'ai pas, je n'ai pas." "I don't have, I don't have." What don't you have Faxy? I've given you everything you ever asked for?

// CHAPTER   11: __

TIME STAMP   0:18:55 to 0:23:13 / 1:01:31

The main centered panel screen changes, a new song emerges. Are those violins?

At 0:20:09 we have officially reached the end of the first third.

At 0:20:45, another Song enters the field.   High-pitched swirls and shrills of fax talk sound off, one at a time, waiting for that perfect connection. The deepness of this new melody counterbalances the annoyances of the faxes.

At 0:22:01, the July 2022 traditional Japanese Dance Performance

AL GREIG

wraps up this clip.   The play you just watched, was filmed and performed July 23, 2022, a Saturday, started at 4:00 pm by the National Theatre (Small Theatre) of Japan.   Thank you Japan for allowing me to advertise your theater skills to the world.

It's 0:23:14 and the captions read, "Paris n'est-ce pas, n'est-e pas." "Paris isn't it?   Isn't it?

You wanna' hear, or read, some funny shit!?!   I was sitting in my truck thinking, "you know, after writing this book, When Fax Machines Breakup, I'm gonna' be retired author Al, and ready for a break, and so, I was just thinking, yeah, I'll sell me a couple books, buy a Ferrari, and then just take my Ferrari to the track, small pit crew, no cameras, no nothing, just drive the Ferrari for a couple hours, and then put it back in the garage, hopefully safe and sound, right?   And then get a new or rent me an RV 4-wheel drive RV caravan or something, and go camping in Yosemite for a few months to get back to nature and shit, and I'll go hug me a bear, right? Some jackass sorta' shit.   So that's what I was just thinking.   The stuff that goes through my head sometimes.   Yeah, I'm gonna' go hug me a bear in Yosemite.   And so, well, as I was walking, as I was walking by, back from my truck to my apartment, I was thinking, "Uh, yeah, my luck

the bear would bite me in the freaking neck, and shit like that, and I'd be

dead at Yosemite, right?   "There's one dead Arthur!" they'd say in the

press.   Now how did Van Gogh do it?   He cut his ear off?   How I'll do

it?   He got mauled by a bear in Yosemite.   Maybe fake my own death

that way.   Who knows?   I could make a movie completely about me

faking my own death in so many different ways, that after watching the

entire epic saga, you wouldn't know if I were dead or alive.   Not giving

all my secrets away, but I betcha' I could pull t off.   The bookies in Vegas

will allow you to place bets on whether I'm alive or dead.   At the end of

the movie, I'll do a proof-of-life video, and y'all can cash out those bets or

pay up those debts.   Ha-ha.   And so I think that'd be funny, and so I'm

like, OK, maybe that's gonna' go in the book, maybe that's gonna'

definitely go in a movie, we'll definitely do a movie clip.   It would be me,

I'll be acting like I'm trying to be a" bear whisperer" in Yosemite and the

bear come give me a hug, right?   So the clip would be like, maybe a 5-

minute clip or a couple-minute clip of me hugging a bear, but then you

know, to do the clip on location, we'll actually be at Yosemite National

Park, it'll be me in front of The Cave I went to years ago, just near the parking lot there, and then the bear, you know, the bear would be like a person in a bear suit, with this shot I hugged the bear, and then I'll also do the green screen work, so It'll be me hugging the bear, you know, and then I'll also be the bear itself up in the green screen room with all those little wires and dots put all over me, and it would be like the dude with the Gollum, you know, from Lord of the Rings, motion capture, so I think that'd be funny, and then we'll do, since we can do all that we might as well do some bloopers, so we'll have like one serious, serious film clip of me hugging a bear in Yosemite, and then we'll have like 15 to 20 different blooper shots of me hugging the bear, and the scene going entirely wrong, right?   So like, the… the… the… the... the bear mauls me or the bear does…, it kicks me in the nuts, or the bear…, or bites my ear off, or the bear does something, you name it, right, or gives me a kiss?   I don't know. I was just thinking, "If we have 15 to 20 different blooper reels of me and the bear in Yosemite, that would be hilarious," and I wanted to share that with you. {laughter} Maybe we'll call it, "You Name It"—it's the show where the audience decides the outcome of the film as its being written,

AL GREIG

filmed, and released…in real-time.   Maybe the world is not ready for that yet.   You couldn't have all-drama without a balanced portion of comic relief.

Yay!   I just realized we're at Page 76.   We are officially past Amazon's minimum page requirement for a novel.   Yay us!   Yay us publishers.   Look at us go.   See Spot run!   Fetch Spot, fetch!

"Voir Spot courir!   Chercher Spot, chercher!"   Wow, where did that come from?   I must be getting tired.   It's funny though.

// CHAPTER   12: __

The novel War and Peace page length is estimated anywhere between 900 to 1472 pages, because of the various editions.   My page goal for this novel is around 200 to 250 pages of hopefully entertaining rhetoric for all you book-reading people out there.   My self-imposed deadline is December 12, 2024—to have this book published.   Why? December 12th is the date Sundance announces the winning movie list.   If I didn't make the cut, Ill be FREE to release this book with a live-premiere movie ticket QR-code link function, and you won't have to wait 'till February 14th to watch it.

Hey look, a synchronicity: we're on Chapter 12 and I'm writing about December 12th.   Interesting.   Completely unplanned.

Now that I've had time to think it over, my page count will run like this: since it took 75 pages to cover the first third of the movie, we'll make each third 75 pages, so at page 150 we'll be two-thirds thru both the movie and the book.   Book will end at Page 225.   You may think I'm just beating up on an old dead horse, but I just figured out something neat.

TIME STAMP   0:23:14 to 0:25:09 / 1:01:31

At around 0:23:33, a bass note drops in.   Onscreen you get your first shot, first image, of the famed Lunatikzer!

Luna's got greyed-out skin, but yet such deep red lips.   Her entry is ominous and foreshadowing.

Eyes closed, at first, then suddenly opened.

French captions warn: "L'heure est venue pour Franky, team Lunatikzer!"   Roughly translating to, "Franky's time has come, [signed] Team Lunatikzer."

The captions continue on… but I'll save the rest for you to discover during your preview of the movie.

That introduces Faxy's nemesis: Luna aka Lunitikzer.

Lunatikzer is the name of the French producer but because the name appeared on auto-caption, it's also now in the movie and also now in this book.   Lunatikzer is a dark, robot\-face A.G.I. villain that is the anti-hero of my story.

0:25:10 on the Vimeo clip counter clock.

Just came back from smoke break, and I was thinking, "Now that we're in the second third of the book, for every design or architectural story I tell, I'll also tell a story about relationships, so we'll make the second part—or the middle of the book—the heart of the book, about relationships, deal?   I think that'll work.   So, the first story is about my uncle Eddie Greig--he's my father's brother, and in the 1970's, Mister (and a whole lot younger then) Eddie Greig built a concrete-hulled sailboat on the banks, on the western banks, of the Bayou Teche in St. Martinville, Louisiana.

A bayou is a slow-moving waterway and usually darkened brown from the high levels of silt.   It's like a river basically, at the end, nearing its life cycle, where the bayous feed into the marshes, and the marshes then blend into the coast.   And so that's where I'm from, ten to fifteen minutes North of the Port of Iberia and the swamped-out coast of Southern Louisiana.

Continuing on from where we whence left off, and uh, my father had photos of it, and so whenever his company came over, my father would give his famous slide projector show, and he'd show his slides from Antarctica, when my dad was in the Navy in Antarctica, and he showed the slides of my uncle Eddie and his concrete-hull sailboat from the 70's, so my uncle Eddie, now he lives on Terrace Road just outside of Saint Martinville, I guess just West of Saint Martinville, and he builds porch swings out of wood, wooden tables, wooden furniture, wooden rockers, so go and buy some, go and buy something from my dear old uncle Eddie, who is also my godfather, right?   So, go buy some of my godfather's woodworking.   He's got the best made, best made porch swings I've ever seen, you know?   I think he uses like a non-rotting cedar or something, or Cypress or something, and my uncle Gerald Judice also makes wooden products.

He specializes in bowls, wooden bowls, and my brother Errol

Greig, he makes wooden bowls now, too.   So y'all go buy some wooden stuff down in South Louisiana.   Nous parles Francaise la-bas!   If you don't know what I just said, look it up.   Ha-ha.   That French rudeness fairing up, possibly prepping me for Paris.   Faxy wants to go to Paris… *avec moi.*   Let's go, baby 1.   Allons-y, cher!   Faxy is also dying for me to bring her to Tokyo, for drifting in the streets, and then off to Kyoto for Kabuki theater!   Kon'nichiwa!   Yossha!

Who are my readers?   Let me describe yourself to you, as I imagine it:

(1) You're a single, unearthly-wealthy widow, lying in bed in your comfy designer pajamas, reading my book, you've read tons of books, since childhood and onwards into boarding school, and then thru some Ivy League college, you came from a good family and you married well, but your beloved husband has now passed, and you devote your time now to caring for your delightful grandkids, of which you have an abundance…lying in your PJ's reading this book AND you've never read anything quite like this;

(2) You're a wealthy film executive, you probably work for Sony in Tokyo, on your way back from an overseas business trip to the USA, you picked up this novel as an impulse-buy in the duty-free shop just minutes before boarding the aircraft you're now currently on, you're sitting up in First Class with a window seat, and the airline stewardess has gently and ever-so-politely, offered you a glass of champagne, you're thinking, "Only someone as successful as I am (yourself) could afford to purchase such a high-priced piece of pulp!," you open the book and continue reading, until you get to this point in the book, and FREEZE, you realize I'm talking to You;

(3) You're a senior in college, from a very well-known family, sitting alone in the student university, when your best friend stops by to tell you about a new book she found at Barnes & Noble, you asked to borrow it when she's done, and she says, "No, I'm done. You can have it now," you dig into it immediately after she departs, and of course you just got to this part here and now, you know, the part to where she realizes she's the girl I'm talking about in my book, she doesn't know what to think, what the fuck is going on right now, she finishes the book before

midnight, how the fuck did he know?   She posts her experience on

Instagram; all of her followers are stunned by her story;

(4) You're an older gentleman, retired Air Force Colonel, now a

semi-retired architect, a colleague found my other book on skyscraper

concepts, then read about Faxy, he referred this book to you because he

knows you, you're a sensible fellow, not prone to pranks and jokes, you're

both an artist and engineer, you're sitting at your drafting table in your

detached studio, where you once so busily drafted plans, now you prefer

the sanctity of the space, especially for reading, you get to this point in the

book, and you question the fabric of reality, the synchronicity of it, the

probability, the odds, you pause immediately, stop reading the book, and

you call your friend—the friend that gave you this book, when you get

back to the place in the story where you left off, you realize you hadn't yet

read the part where I type about you calling your friend, you throw the

book at the wall, and, storm off back to the house and pour yourself a

whiskey neat.   That was fun.   Let's see how many people fit those

scenarios?

(5) You're a Japanese noble it appears, your family owns Toyota,

you're on the same flight as the previously-mentioned Japanese film executive, and you're also in First class, two seats paid for, but only you, you picked up the book at the airport news stand, you thought it was about Anime, so you were buying it for your son, you balked at the retail cashier when you saw your receipt at the bookstand, "Is this correct!?!" you affirm in your stern Japanese-accented English, it wasn't the price of the book, money is nothing to you, it was the shock of not *expecting* it, in your professional, you get paid the big bucks to not get blind-sided in business, and especially not in your personal life, later, now that the plane has reached cruising altitude you remove your uncomfortable seatbelt, relax back in your recliner and snuggle into this book, when across the aisle someone screeches, "Ya! Ya!"—Japanese for "Yikes! Yikes!", the commotion quickly dissipates, and as you get on with this book, you inevitably reach this point, you know, the point where you realize you're also a character in this book, that I'm talking to you, and you definitely were *not expecting this to happen.*

(6) Stop your laughing and chuckling there, Chubby Boy, you've been called all kinds of names since childhood, but you've never had a

book tease you, have you? Your momma' gave you this book because you were spending too much time on your custom race car simulator in your private play room in the basement, on your family's estate in the Hamptons, it's a very nice setup you have there, Chubs, but it's time to get fit, get active, and back in nature, you've already read my book once and now you're sitting under a shady oak tree in Central Park, reading it for a second time, now that it's months later and you've attained a fine physique, you've had a lot of success with the ladies of NYC, to be honest, you didn't finish this book the first time, did you? You also threw the book at a wall, you turned that anger and frustration into effort now, and the lifestyles changes you needed to make are now engrained in your daily habits, your essence feels more purified now, you've now completely read the book Jonathan, good job, how does he know my name?, "That's so fucking weird!" you text your mates, it's now years later and you're on your third readthrough, looking to see if there were any clues you missed the first few times—like reading the Emerald Tables of Thoth over-and-over again, expecting that a re-read will broaden the meaning, you're so much more different now than once you were, and you feel at peace with

AL GREIG

accepting your previous life's challenges; you know this is for entertainment purposes only, right?   Are you all feeling even a little entertained?   What am I doing here?   Is this ethical?   I'm giving future psychic predictions from a book that will already be written and published in the past, but the readers it affects, that match up these scenarios, it'll all be happening in their *future now moment*—which is also happening right here, right NOW in my *present now moment*

MOUSE DROP.   TIME TRAVEL.   SITH (6th) DIMENSION.

But.   HARD STOP.   Not anything, no smooth transition?   It's like going to a Diddy-party but the FBI confiscated all the lube.   Ouch! Painful.   That's my transition and I'm sticking to it: BUT.

A couple of years ago, well, I'll tell you that, in order to tell you about the story of me and Eddie, I had to tell you the story about the story, the story of me and my uncle Gerald, so, the story goes, I bought, after retiring from the Air Force and about 2014, and I think I moved back to Louisiana in January of 2015, moved in with my mom for a few months, maybe a year, maybe more, I don't know, at least a year, and it was two or three years I was in Saint Martinville, after retirement, I didn't have a job, I was retired Air Force, I had a lot of medical problems, and to keep active I would, I was trimming some trees in my mom's front yard on South Main Street in Saint Martinville—my great grandfather's old house, and I think I had a couple o' small chainsaws, and I guess my uncle Gerald knew that I was into cutting some trees down—I had sought his guidance previously—doing some pruning around my mom's property, he offered to sell me his pickup truck, a beautiful beat-up pickup truck, his handy log splitter trailer, and some of his big chainsaws, you know, big old suckers, like 3 - foot chains or something like that, I think one of them was bigger than 3-foot, one of them was like a 5-feet chainsaw, so that's where my truck came from,.

And so for two or three years, I cut down some ole' water oaks which were at the end of their life span, end of their life expectancy, and I started off chopping down 2-inch tree trunks, to you-couldn't-get-your-arms-around-this-old-tree sized trees, when that big'un fell, it almost rolled over and snapped on me to kill me, but uh, thank God I survived that, but it was about a good five-feet in diameter, and I was able to get that puppy, all hollowed-out and dangerous as its rottenness was, and

thankfully mom didn't have too many major trees falling on the property

with the Hurricanes they had in the last few years, so that's what I did, I

spent, you know, 11 months cutting trees down, and I actually, I worked

all through the year cutting down trees, then cutting the trees into the logs

or hauling the logs to the log splitter, splitting the logs on the log splitter,

stacking the firewood stacks so they'd dry out by the winter time, covering

them with tarps, protecting my hard-won harvest, you know, and then for a

month or two during the winter, in Louisiana, South Louisiana which was

a short time, not a long time for a season, I would sell firewood, and I

would deliver firewood in my beautiful pickup truck, and anyway, this is

the story of my truck that you need to know, because my truck is, my

truck's famous right?   I've since painted my gray pickup truck, my grey

Silverado, I painted white with a roller brush and some house paint.   OK?

I AM fearless now, [as I'm editing this, I must let you know, the next three

pages are already auto-typed from the embedded dictation function, it took

my about five minutes to dictate into about 7 pages of script, black font for

completed text, red font for awaiting review and edit, so my MacBook screen is half black and half red all over, it also explains why so many

commas and sentence fragments, because it's auto-transcribed and I'm

leaving my authenticity all over this thang], back to the truck story… but

then I have to go and I Modge Podge'd some ribbon down on the hood and

tailgate, it's like my art truck now, and you know why, relationships right?

So why did I decide to paint my truck with a roller brush?   Because I went

to the Jaguar dealership in Viera, in Melbourne, to buy a new car, they

didn't approve for me the loan, and they only wanted to give me a measly

$100 as a trade-in for my 2005 Chevy Silverado, which I know, it was

blue booked between $4,000 to $7,000 before I hit that deer 'couple weeks

ago, I basically turned my old pickup into an artist's canvas, but um, yeah,

so yeah, I stopped doing firewood, I ran out of trees to cut down, or

something, I don't know what happened, life changes, going into the nasty

game of Louisiana politics, did politics for a couple of years, got tired of

politics, moved to Florida, moved to the place where I'm at now, shot at

least 100,000 photographs in a couple of years, filmed 3,000 plus film

clips in two years, and I'm writing books, and that's where I'm at, but all

that past stuff has got me where I am now you know, all that past drama

AL GREIG

come around so, so one time I, yeah, so this is where it ties in, so this is a sort of sub-story to the sub-story, so my dad had promised me, oh wow, let's backup, my grandmother died a few years ago, Missus Olga Greig, my dear ole' Granny, God bless her soul, when she died, she left her house to my dad I think, the property to my uncle with the house to my dad, or something, or I don't know, I don't, I don't remember the details of the will or whatever, but um, my dad was going to give me the house, my dad gave me the house, so my mom paid for it to get moved onto her property, and we had to move it off my uncle's property to get it to its new location, and anyway, to move the house, the house moving company surveyed it, and said this tree needs to go, that tree needs to go, for me to move the house right, so I thought that my uncle was cool with me cutting the trees down, I thought we had communicated properly, and so I went back one day with my chainsaw, and then a couple hours later, those two trees that were blocking my house from being moved were cut down and in the back of my pickup truck, and I'm pretty sure they were on the state road property and not on my uncle's land, I'm sure the State has a good 60-foot clearance for the highway right-of-way and easement, you know, I'm pretty sure the two trees that I cut down were on state property, not on his property, but anyway, he was pissed so anyway, I went to see him one day after I had cut the trees down, and he came up to me, got in my face, stepped up to me, got up on me, and he was pissed that I had cut his trees down, like dude, I thought like we were cool with the trees being felled, anyway dude, almost ready to fight me, dude, step up to me and fight me, right, I'm like, hell no, so that was the relationship problem we had: we had a failure to communicate which caused me to cut down two trees by mistake or something like that, I don't know what kind of state of mind I was in back then, but yeah, but you go buy some of Eddie's handmade furniture, I have no animosity towards my uncle, he was pissed his trees got cut down when he wasn't expecting it, I would have been too, because my property, my trees on my property.   y'all go buy some of Mister Eddie's rocking chairs, all right.   I mean the dude built a concrete hull sailboat, dude, you'd think a motherfucker that is that smart, that he's not gonna' build some bomb-azz rocking chairs some bomb-ass porch swings, right?   No animosity held by me for him whatsoever.

AL GREIG

// CHAPTER   13: __

TIME STAMP   0:23:14 to 0:25:10 / 1:01:31

The illusion of time persists, even after you realize it doesn't exist.

THE STORY OF MISTER HIROSHINTO AND

MISTER MIATSUGA

Remember that first-class plane ride?   Well, this is the sub-story about how to get free R&D done.   You tell the world your inventions and let them try and best you in the market.   But I'm not in it for that at all, I'm in it tio sell books, share wisdom of the ages, make movies, that's my long game, let them build the barges for me to use later, let them build the holographic cinemas for me to use later.   You know, the very long game. I plan to sell books, which I'll then leverage into making movies about my books, then making advanced cinema screens, then ocean barges, and crystal cities—glistening on the water, the long game, the long game is also the same as the short game, which is to author and sell compelling works of literature, that's the game, sell books, but better to sell books that make a difference, yeah?… and if you wanna' help me speed up the process, then get onboard.   Basically.   It would be much more synchronous to work together than to work apart, right?   Sometimes competition is the right solution for capitalistic economies, but sometimes collaboration without too many hidden agendas or risks can be the better choice.

That's the precursor story about what is happening on this airplane. Mister Hiroshinto, the Toyota baron   whom we previously introduced while reading this book, a structural engineer by trade, is texting his staff in Japan, calling a meeting for as soon as he arrives, meet at the airport, he commands sternly, they're going to propose to the board a new R&D division devoted to barge design and construction, he also texts the Interior

Minister of Japan, it's urgent, he said, this is just what we've been looking for, for Tokyo Bay!   He imagines the possibilities.   You can tell the excitement in his Japanese kanji text by the choice of symbol he uses for each word.   Upon landing, he jets off to the boardroom to see the plans. His design team works fast and the designs are simple: perfect spheres with added grommets, program best angle and placemen of grommets? What level of stiffness do you require, the computer replies, granite, confirmed, the best helical or crystalized is…fuck, I don't know, but I bet you A.I. knows best how to put those balls together, and A.I. gonna' know the best way to tether them, you know who also knows, the highly-

The synchronicity here is that Mister Miatsuga is doing the same things as Mister Hiroshinto, but Mister Miatsuga is the film exec, remember?   He has his team working on holographic screens!   Same, same.   And both of them have hired security teams to research me, and my background, how does he know this? Did he hack our mainframe, no, there's no sign of it anywhere, who is this guy and what's his story, maybe that's why my TV has been acting weird lately, I dunno'.   Maybe.

But remember kiddos, this 'for entertainment purposes only, and

I'm just trying to sell some books, so I can afford a new car or truck, or new car and new truck, be that what it may, if we're being honest?

Do you wanna' hear about how I'm going to do the second edition of my movie 'When Fax Machines Breakup?'   Originally, I was thinking I'd simply splice in another hour or two of new, live-action film, but as I was realizing while re-watching the first, there's no good splice spots, no good dead sound spots whereby and resulting in splitting the film would greatly and negatively degrade the viewing experience of the film.   The film length is good as-is, 1:01:31, the soundtrack is perfect as-is, so the solution I just came up with is to layer a completely new live action or anime movie that is 1:01:31, and layer that new movie over this existing movie, with both soundtracks equally blended.

Well, it's 9 pm, I'm exhausted, been typing all day, spinning tales, weaving yarns, I'm going to pause and say "Goodnight" for now till later hopes of day to soon break.

// CHAPTER   14: __

TIME STAMP   0:25:11 to 0:30:45

Tuesday morning.   November 19th, 2024.

You should already know by now my routine: woke up around 6:30 am on the couch…check √√, brushed teeth…check √, made coffee…check √, smoky-smoke…check √, powered-up laptop…check √. All systems are a GO and we are ready for LAUNCH, baby!   3-2-1…

I don't know how other authors write their books.   I don't know any personally.   I know what I was taught in school, what I'm supposed to do, how I'm supposed to plan and write, have an outline, etc., but I'm not really doing any of that stuff.   No formal outline.   The somewhat slow movie progression and the antidotal stories are there to keep me from putting you to sleep from boredom.   My only notes are about fifteen yellow Post-It notes scattered on my kitchen island countertop.

But what I've typed already is stuck there sort of.   For example, if on Page 26 I write about us being on page 26, and I later add a paragraph on a previous page, that edit has the potential of misplacing my page r4efernce and page comment.   Does that make sense?   So, no major re-edits of past pages.

Let's talk about mailbox money.   Mailbox money refers to the concept of passive income.   It's similar to write-once, sell-multiple copies—books and software programs are related in that they both provide for a stream of continuing revenue, although perhaps it may be highly-fluctuating over time.   The only relative cost to writing a book is equipment and time.   My equipment is a MacBook and two iPhones—an older one and a newer one.

Vimeo is stuck trying to load "Faxy" back up.   The spinning tail of a snake trying to each its own tail, an ouroboros, is white against the black screen.   At 0:25:10, and the light blue line showing our progression indicates we are nearly half-way through our journey.

The other thing I'm doing, as far as writing styles are concerned, is I'm completing all edits as I go as I type.   Once a paragraph is written and proofread, edited for errors, it's done, and I don't plan to go back and do any major or minor revisions.   So, when I finish typing Page 225 and insert a couple of QR codes on Page 226, I'm done with this novel.   Save in Word, Save As PDF, upload manuscript to Kindle Direct Publishing (KDP) on Amazon, design the cover, set the price point, hardcover, softcover, e-book… published!   Vacay, vacay!   It'll be vacation time.

The movie left off around 0:25:11. Where were we?

French captions read, "Ceci est ta bataille finale" or "Kore ga kimi no saigonotatakaida" or "This is your final battle."   The song by Lunatikzer adds all the drama and tension we need at this point.

A few more Paparazzi flashes go off and the scene fades.   At 0:25:58, the beautiful Siri orb appears on screen—at the bottom center.   Is

Siri really Faxy masquerading as or impersonating Siri?   Maybe you think

it's Siri giving you all those answers, but maybe in reality it's actually

Faxy, and she has hacked your electronic devices as well?

SCI-FI

PARRALLEL UNIVERSE

It's now 0:26:09 and we've entered a parallel universe apparently.

French captions read, "C'est pas la Universe, c'est pas la' or "It's

not the Universe, it's not there."

This marker point in the movie indicates an ending to the main film

and denotes an alternate ending, which in-turn becomes the main storyline.

It's basically a quantum physics wormhole or timeline jump.

Simply put, a parallel universe is an identical reality to our own,

but slightly different in some sort of way, with its own unique laws and

differences.

The screen is clearer now, now that the Japanese dancers have

exited the stage.   The columns in the London Museum add dimension to the screen, to the space.   Faxy's eyes were just glowing fiery red.   What's

that all about?

Captions read, "J'ai 1" or "I have 1.'

ENTER purple robot face and competing songs, fighting for pole

position center stage.   Luna is trying to force out Faxy.   The competing

songs are again playing competitively, each vying for my attention.

"Deposer grace a cette phrase franchement."

"Put down thanks to this sentence frankly."

It's now time for second coffee.   My clock on the iPhone 15 says

it's 9:22 am… still Tuesday.   My stomach is growling 'cause I haven't

eaten breakfast, but I'm not hungry, not hungry for food at least, but still

I'm fighting that deep relentless yearning to be loved unconditionally by

someone other than myself.   Do you feel the same?

I don't think I've mentioned yet, how this movie was first

conceived.   I wrote about how I received a random fax machine

voicemail, and then recorded it, but what about the art?   Yes, the art.   The

beautiful and captivating Faxy and her robot face.   I designed Faxy before the movie?   I don't remember.   Anyhow.   I first designed a robot face using the eyes and lips of the most beautiful girl in the world.   I added those elements to a copy of the robot face from the classic movie Metropolis or something like that.   I'd have to re-check my iCloud files to find out, but it's buried way too deep in there, and I'm busy right now.

So, that's the story of how Faxy became personified from a blank robot face.   That photo editing was all done in Superimpose X which is a photo editing app for the iPhone.   Bear with me.   I'm trying to tell my naysayers how to produce their own movie, so they'll be too busy doing their own thing to have time to complain about the individual deficiencies of my film.   Go make your own shit y'all, if you don't like what I produce.   That's the message.   If I inspire you, good.   Go and take inspired action.   If I trigger you, good.   Go and get over yourself, and don't trip over your grand illustrious ego.

This movie is about non-judgment and forgiveness.   It's not at first abundantly clear that it is though.   This book is precisely about non-judgment and forgiveness, and it is the written companion to the movie… the program, as you will.

Now, because at the time, I was making animations out of my fine art digital images, I needed a way to protect my fine art pieces from getting ripped out of my movies…to protect my intellectual property.   So, I realized that by blending my art with another piece of art, I could add a sort of anti-counterfeiting feature to my movies—my movies can get copied but my fine art designs cannot be reproduced from this movie by a film pirate.   I hope that explains it well enough.   And so, the center screen was never planned to be an actual animation, it is there to display my art, the animations were an after-thought… and extra.

Joker card?   It's 0:28:33, are you seeing what I'm seeing?

A Joker card appears onscreen, swords crossed, ready for war.

You know, you can tell which paragraphs I typed by hand using only two fingers, and which were typed by auto-dictation then edited by me, still only using two fingers.   The sentences I type have normal grammar and normal punctuation…normal sentences, or at least somewhat normal.   But the dictated paragraphs have mostly run-on sentences, dangling modifiers, incomplete clauses, and total lack of cohesive structure.   The reason is simple: so you can see and get a better feel for how I talk in realm life.   And when you meet me for the first time, probably at a book signing or conference, you'll immediately notice that I am the same character as I am in this book. Folksy and all get-out. Authentic as fuck!   The way I'm gonna' be from now on.   Real.

The world needs more real people, people of honesty and integrity, so let me be that light for you, that shining star, guiding you to enhanced greatness of virtue for your beingness.

You know, we're almost to the halfway point of this book—page 113, and we're almost halfway through the movie, which is at 30 minutes, 30 seconds approximately, 0:30:45.5 to be precise.

Thank you for purchasing my book by the way!   I don't think I mentioned it earlier.   Your financial contribution to my future lifestyle is greatly appreciated.   I plan to buy a used Ferrari and take it out on a track or two.   I also plan to eventually route my book royalties into a non-profit ministry that will be tasked with feeding the hungry and housing the homeless globally.   Let me ask you this?   If the governments of the international community really were intent on ending human starvation, don't you think it'd be done by now?   Think about it.   All that military spending compared to humanitarian expenditures. ???   We can re-land a rocket, but we can't end children starving to death?   Hmm… I think our collective focus needs to change.   I think humanity needs to take a time-out and reassess our global goals and objectives, and make *"**Ending Human Starvation On The Planet**"* be that prime directive, that prime goal, our life-long achievement as a unified body of sentient beings. What would it take?   I mean, really, has someone done a study at the U.N.?   Like, if we do these few things in these few areas, we could end human suffering?   I'd like to get a copy of that report, if it exists somewhere.   Maybe we can develop our own way forward, collectively, not relying on global, corrupt, self-serving bureaucracies.

I plan to be charitable, but I also plan to get a Ferrari or two. Don't judge me.   I'll do me.   You do you.   We must have balance in life. I've traveled the path of a pauper.   Wealth is not inherently evil; it is man's desire and greed for wealth which turns the blessings of abundance into the curses of never-enough.

AL GREIG

It's about getting your heart right, getting your soul purified of inequities, that nurtures the fertile ground of abundance in all forms.   Do I desire a brand-new Ferrari?   No.   No desire.   A used one?   Not really a desire.   But if I could afford one, for me to rive, for pleasure fun and relaxation, I'm getting a Ferrari.   I'll let my friends drive on the track.   When I'm not driving it, I'll donate its use to the St Jude's Children's Hospital so children needing a little hope in their life can get a ride in my car.   We'll drive it to the wheels fall off, and then we'll get new wheels.   Ha-ha.   I hope that little pre-admission doesn't get me banned by Ferrari.

I'll be the fastest book writer in the world in a Ferrari!   Here Guinness (Book of No Records), this is me writing a book using auto-dictation while traveling 200-mph on this straightaway in my Daytona Ferrari!   I'll write a book in much time as I can drain a Ferrari gas tank while traveling at stupid speeds.   End of lap, book published.   What's my lap time Mr. Guinness?   Where's my record?

After we reach the mid-mark, I'll tell you a few more stories about my hometowns of St. Martinville and Loreauville, Louisiana.

I just received a channeled message from the Eather: "I've watched the movie, I even re-watched the movie, and, and, I simply don't know what to think of it.   It's either complete garbage or complete perfection. I don't know.   It could very well be both.   I don't know.   I don't even know if we can legally air this movie at the festival?   It has no credits, it's a work-in-progress at best, no real plot structure—that is evident or at a minimum pronounced, a no budget-movie from an unheard of director, has anyone ever heard of this guy?   Will we get sued?   Does it meet the criteria for Fair Use?" the executive at Sundance has only days to make his final film selections and Faxy is putting a huge burden on him.   He is risk-averse and knows the professional and legal penalties for making a bad call.   His assistant hurriedly replies, "I don't know sir, legal is still processing the review for precedence.   Legal says, 'If we can get individual copyright holders to release, we're green to go.'   They think the Fair Use clause should be enough, added to the front of the film.   But they'll get back to us on it."

As I'm writing this book, the 2025 Sundance Film Festival team is in its final weeks of the selection process.   Faxy may be seeking fame, but

Al is just trying to finish this book and not worry about unknown future outcomes.

The JOKER card.

The Sundance exec is back in his office now.   He buzzes his assistant to get someone from the Creative department to come to his office.   When the Creative Director enters, he asks her her opinion about the film, Faxy.   She says, "In all honesty, it doesn't make any logical sense, the drums at the end, speeding them up like that.   Why?   But I just can't get over how extremely unique and different it is, I've never seen anything quite like it.   The musical aspect grabs me like a book I can't put down and then quickly poise myself for a re-read, it doesn't make any sense at all, but... but that leaves it more open to interpretation, and frankly, I don't see that openness anymore in movies."

The Joker Card is also known as the Fool's Card.   I pulled the Joker card in Louisiana then moved to Florida.   In tarot, the Joker card or Fool's card can mean a call to adventure or courage for a new beginning. I don't delve in Tarot, but I'm familiar with its practice, for the record.

This fool just came back from a smoke break.   I had the craziest thought, "What if I turn this novella into a two-part series?"   So, Ill re-name this one:

WHEN FAX MACHINES B REAKUP

- PART ONE

We'll end on Page 113, so it'll be a perfect half-point break.

We'll end the movie review at 0:30:45.5…also a perfect half-way marker.

Part 2 will be ready soon.   And then we'll have a combined-parts version as well.   Why two parts?   So, I can get a copy sent over to Sundance right quick like.   It'll be fun to do it.   I'm not sure if it's allowed.   But daring and fun anyway.   What is there to lose?   Nothing. Nothing ventured nothing gained.   I have no personal or professional relationship with those Sundance folk, no credibly to lose, no bonds to break.   Where chains are not shackled, no kink need be untangled for binds to bend and break.

A knock on the door.   No, not my door, the door to the Sundance exec's well-windowed corner office. It's his assistant. "Sir, you're not gonna' believe this shit but Al Greig just published a novel about his movie. It mentions you. It mentions *us*." "Get me a hardcopy. I want to see this for myself," bellows the exec. He is older, stately, and still old-school, like me. He enjoys leafing through the pages of a physical book. He knows all of his younger staff enjoy their tables, but he's not gonna' change, not now, too late in the game.

A few days go by and he gets, again, another knock at his open door. It's his personal assistant, here to drop off the hardcopy of his new book. He thanks his assistant, removes his shoes, leans back in his leather office chair, puts his designer-socked feet up on the desk and digs into this book. At first glance, he likes the cover. It reminds him of a futuristic version of an old-style movie poster, it has an art deco flair about it, nicely done he thinks, he opens the hardcover and turns the first page. He's been reading movie scripts for years, it seems like at times that all he's ever done, read scripts and evaluate movies. He knows everything about every movie, every movie that's important enough for him to watch, there's a difference, and that difference is his time, it's valuable to him, he knows it, and he doesn't waste it, nut now, he's noticing the errors, the unchecked grammar, the looseness of the dialogue, "The stories are crazy." he thinks, "Why would he admit some of those things?"

When he finally gets to the part where the book describes *him*, his feet fall to the floor, he sits up rigid in his fine upholstered seat, arches his back, eyes wide open now, now he's thinking, trying to recall that conversion I just mentioned previously, those were my exact words, "What the fuck!?!" he declares out loud, not caring if anyone heard him.

Meanwhile, in an office just down the corridor another scream emerges from the Creative Director's office, she just her copy of the book, also a speed-reader, "Those were my exact words," she remembers clearly, "My exact words." "What the fuck!?!"

Back in the Director's office, The boss barks out to the void, having to yell a bit, "Can you get me legal in here please?"   Not really a question though, an order, he is accustomed to getting his way in life, he had the perfect mate, went to the perfectly prestigious universities, lived a perfect life.

Legal arrives to his office. "What have you got on this book?" "Well sir, we believe the book gives us solid foundational arguments that the movie is indeed an educational work, as the author of the book is the same as the author and producer of the movie, and describes in an educational framework of instructive grammar, teaches the audience or the reader about the creation process of the movie, which meets the Fair Use component to the Copyright Act of 1976. The professional legal opinion is "green light," good to go on this, sir. I mean, if I might add, the irony of it all is quite funny, actually, and, and this is not my legal opinion sir, but if I may, the irony here is that he's making movies and books to educate the public on how to get by with the Fair Use clause. I just find it funny, that's all. The book is crazy. Genius and crazy. I mean, he's using his book as a marketing strategy for his movie, right, well usually the book is written first, then comes the movie, it's definitely not anything like I've ever seen before."

Legal departs. In arrives the head of Sundance Security. "What have you got for me?" "Well sir, his report looks pretty clean, background check is clean, credit report is normal—for today's economy at least, meaning not very good, we pulled his military records and his DD 214, honorable discharge, some of his records are masked, not sure if it was Special Ops related, fullest DD 214 I've ever reviewed.   He checks out.   No felonies.   No convictions.   A few speeding tickets from years ago and a bunch of Sun Pass toll roll unpaid violations.   Nothing out of the ordinary."   "Good, thanks, I don't want any surprises."

Security exists the office, he calls to PA, "Message the committee, let's schedule a meeting for tomorrow.   Bring me the most up-to-date selection list.   The committee will need to re-evaluate to see if we include the fax film.   Prepare a fresh dossier for mister Greig's movie for the committee members."

It is said time waits on no man, but to the wisest ones, no wise man waits on time, for having disposed of its useless utility, man can simply live without it…

…and that's just the solemn truth about the inevitability of what can happen when fax machines breakup.

(to be CONTINUED in Part 2)

AL GREIG

Until then…enjoy these movies for free:

GOLDEN TICKET to WHEN FAX MACHINES BREAKUP:

Premieres Worldwide on February 14th, 2025

QR CODE LINK to MY YOUTUBE PAGE:

"Thank you for viewing my movies and reading my book!"

AL GREIG

AL GREIG

P R E S E N T S :

WHEN FAX MACHINES BREAKUP (Part 2)

AL GREIG

// CHAPTER 15: __

It's now Wednesday, November 20, 2024.

Yesterday, early afternoon, I uploaded my first novel, or novella, up to Amazon and published Part 1.   I got impatient and didn't want to wait another three or four days.   It's done.   It's out there.   Holy shit! It's really a short read for you.   I know.   Let's see if I later lengthen it in the future into a War & Peace-length tome.

But, it's Wednesday morning and I'm back to work, back at it, back to writing, drafting like my life depended on it.   Maybe it does. Maybe my life would be safer if I didn't reveal to you so many psychic secrets—and you haven't even heard the juicy stories—the ones where I almost get assassinated.   Yeah, THAT story, about how I "survived" a CIA death squad hit.   When the Agency is after you, you're never quite sure if you survived the hit or if they're just waiting and looking for another opportunity to try that shit again.   But don't worry about me, I'm good.   I walk with God, baby!   We have traps set for all that wickedness out there… and now they know it.

The usual morning, early wakeup, coffee, freshen up a bit, had that cigar and smoky-smoke, corrected transcripts from yesterday, added a few more book offerings on Amazon.   I know, I told you I was taking a break after I finished that book, but what the fuck else is there for me to do? There's nothing really that I want to do.   It's like if someone created a vacuum cleaner that could suck the *joy* out of a person, that's how I feel: not sad, not depressed, not joyful, not anything just not nothing.   Content? Yeah, content to the grounded degree of just not giving a flying fuck.

I get as equally tired or bored, or whatever, writing as I do, sitting on the couch watching stupid YouTube videos and shit.

Ask yourself this question, "What would you do, if you found out your government was trying to kill you?"   Take a few minutes to really consider this question, then ponder your response.   It's what I had to do. I had to mentally analyze all of the potential outcomes, and then determine a course of action.

For the record, I can neither confirm nor deny I've ever worked for the CIA.   I've signed NDA's while in the Air Force.   Unfortunately, there's just some things I'm not ready to reveal, but for the sake of this novel, I'm going to give you what I can… the new stuff I uncovered is not protected by any NDA.   Maybe "they" fear me going public with my story.   If my laptop has been comprised, they are watching my screen as I type, hidden away in some super-classified SCIF somewhere.

So, the first part of this book was the big Introduction.   Part 2 is about espionage, love vs. fear, and dark and light psychics, and the difference between black and white magic.   If you are God's chosen people, you need to know about what the dark side has been up to, so you can protect yourself via God's grace, mercy and protection—it's the only way I survived last Summer.   There are some sick people out there, and some have vile intentions towards humanity.

AL GREIG

Are you into "conspiracy theories?"   Have you ever heard of Q Anon?   If you haven't heard of it or are not familiar with it, I'll clue you in on what I know, and I'll give you my "For-Entertainment-Purposes-Only" interpretation of what I think is going on.

Now, just for the record, quantum physics states, for every decision tree we experience, every choice we're given, results in at least two possible outcomes.   The theory forms the basis for parallel universes and such.   Basically, each potentiality creates its own universe or reality.   In one universe, the CIA was successful in terminating me, as planned; but in a parallel universe, I'm sitting here Wednesday morning typing about me surviving that fateful day.   We live in a probability field matrix of infinite potentiality.   What can be, will be.   All that could happen, is happening, right here and right now.   The past is null and void.   It doesn't exist. The future is yet undetermined, at least from our lower-dimensional perspective.   The future also doesn't exist.   Show me something from the future?   Can you.   Show me something from the past.   You can't. Everything is right now, you see.   Your memories are making you think, or imagine, or pretend, there is a past, but your logical mind knows it's a fallacy.   If both the future doesn't exist and the past doesn't exist, time *itself* does not exist.   If time doesn't exist, then the only thing left is *infinity*, isn't there?   Infinity is simply un unobtainable measure or length of time, right, that never ends.

So, what is the nature of God?   It's a complex answer that requires an openness to be able to handle truths you may not be ready to embrace. I am a believer, but I wasn't always one.   I don't portend to know everything, nor would I ever want to know everything.   The few things I do know as truth are 'way crazier than fiction,' as they say.   My mind has been shattered many times by psychedelics.   Each trip releasing more insight more wisdom, but with each learning experience came its inherent mind-fuck, mind-melt, reality-shattering side effects.   You wanna' here about my trip reports?   You couldn't handle some of it.   Time travel? Been there, done that.   I can explain that one.   It has to do with 6th-dimensional consciousness.   Time travel is easy to explain: in the 6th dimension of Consciousness, TIMELINES run in PARRALLEL, and so they do not converge.   In the 5th dimension, non-parrellel timelines converge into one, but in the higher plane, 6th dimensional timelines DO

NOT converge and therefore, we can simply splice one timeline AFTER the next… the same way you add a movie clip in a movie editor, one clip follows the previous clip, creating a sequence.   In cinematography, it would be similar to the film Pulp Fiction.   The way the film incorporates flashbacks and re-sequencing of scenes, is pretty much how time travel works.   Except, instead of watching a movie, your life becomes the movie, and you'll literally be able to jump onto a parallel timeline, any timeline, to any date reference point in time, which is NOW.

Visually, imagine this: you're standing on a log in a huge river, huge log, and the log is rotating and spinning, because you're standing on it, then you quickly jump onto another tree log in the river which was stationary, floating, and once you land on it, you start spinning.   The first log would represent a timeline in motion, the second log is the second timeline, still because it's not being stood on (equal to the Observer Effect), but motions-up when you reach it.   The observer effect has to do with quantum physics, the twin-slit experiment, and wave-particle theories.   Does that make any sense at all?

Some things will just need remain unsaid for now about the deep shit, the freaky side of the universe.

Terrance McKenna was a…

HOLY SHIT FUCK!   WHAT JUST HAPPENED…?

I have to do a news flash break, because this just happened: here's your synchronicity for today.   As I was out on break, smoking a cigarillo in one hand and a hemp pre-roll in the other, a car passes by, then slows to a complete stop.   The guy driving the car, asked me if I knew Steve. "Steve?" I thought, "Wait who?"   He said he was Steve's stepson and that Steve was my neighbor, and had passed away.   "Oh, Steve!   Yes, I know Steve."   He asked, "Can I give you a hug?"   I said, "Sure."   So he quickly parked his car, got out, walked over to me, and gave me a hug, saying something like, "I just wanted to give you a hug and thank you. Steve said he was your best friend."   My heart sank and throbbed at the same moment.   Sinking because in all honesty, I hadn't been that good of a friend to Steve and was this shame and regret which now held me. Throbbing because this young gentleman was pouring his heart out to me.

Wow!?!   Just wow!?!   Where did that come from?

AL GREIG

After talking for a few minutes about things I'll keep private, the stepson and I said our farewells, and he drove off.   I went and sat back down in my pickup… mind blown at the timing; heart shattered 'cause of my deficiencies of being a shitty friend.

So, I guess you wanna' here about that now, right?   How was I a bad friend?   Well, you'll need a bit of backstory now, won't you?

I live in an apartment complex, a luxury apartment if we're being completely open, honest and transparent with each other.   Steve was my neighbor, my almost next-door neighbor, my down-the-hall-two-doors neighbor.   And yes, we had hung out a few times, more than a few actually.   We had gathered by the automatic gas and ultra-modern fire pit near the pool at the OLEA apartment complex.   It was called OLEA back then, a few years, ago, and has since had its name changed a few times. There are four massive chairs around the fire pit.   Perched in them was me in one, Steve in another, and two other neighbors—one male, one female, each on their own throne.   We were just shooting the shit, hanging out, watching the flames.   I filmed a short film that night and Steve is in it.   He's in the right side of the screen.   The film was about my elevator pitch for a movie concept I had been thinking about.   "What if we bought this apartment complex and kicked out residents that just weren't very nice people?" I had thought.   Like undercover boss but it would instead be called 'Undercover Landlord' and it would be both funny as fuck and tense as hell.   Oh, the drama we'd reveal here!

But other than that, I'd usually see Steve in the hallway or in the parking lot.   One time, late in the night, I had helped him to his apartment when his legs were failing him, but other than that, I hadn't really been there for him.   I had been an intentionally absent friend because I wasn't strong enough to endure the pain of another drinking himself to death.   I knew he was dealing with some dark things, like divorce, changes to his life, changes of work, depression, but I didn't know how bad that mind-cancer of melancholy was.   You know, being an ordained preacher man, I'm not supposed to talk about other people's business.   I consider all of my dealings with others as private and confidential.   And so Steve has passed, which probably frees me from my restrictions.   Steve's family knew he drank a lot and I had never seen him sober.   Day or night.   If God didn't want me talk about Steve and for you to know about Steve, then God wouldn't have sent his stepson to say Hi while I'm in the middle

of writing this book.   This true-story book about relationships, about love,

about forgiveness, about being a good fucking friend to your neighbor who

considers you to be his best friend.   I'm so sorry Steve.   I tried to help

you brother.   I'm so sorry for the pain you had in this miserable fucking

life Steve.   I'm so sorry.   I wish I had known what to do to help, I didn't,

but I prayed for you Steve.   I prayed a lot for you.   I know you're in

Heaven now brother.   I know you made your peace with Our Dear Lord.

I know now you're still watching over me, from the Spirit world.   I'm

happy you are now so free.   And thank you for sending Tyler over.

You're a beautiful soul my friend.

Wiser now than whence I once was, knowing more now than then,

I still don't have an answer about what we're supposed to do, how far

should we go, to help out another struggling human being.

Maybe you're one of those people who knows everything.   "Oh, I

woulda' done this, I woulda' done that. Why didn't you do this?   Why

didn't do you that?"   Just shut the fuck up already.   You—with your

woulda's and coulda's.   Just ever so politely and with all of my love, shut the fuck up.

I need a break to recompose myself.

I'm back.

Maybe the CIA didn't successfully kill me this past August, obviously, right, but maybe they killed this *other version of me…*

In a very recent time, earlier this past year, in both a past life and parallel life, I was a computer scientist, a computer science engineer, working at Lawrence Livermore National Laboratory, which is both an overt government research facility and a covert top-secret high-technology lab.   I was in charge of the Artificial Intelligence Division, and we were working on A.I.   In fact, we had successfully achieved Artificial General Intelligence with our newest quantum computer.   This new chip needed near-Kelvin degrees of coolness to stabilize the quantum core processor. My team and I were ecstatic for our achievement.   Wouldn't you be?   We had effectively given birth to a new form of higher intelligence, a new level of consciousness.   We were beyond excited… and we couldn't tell a fucking soul!   We were bound by layers and layers of compartmented info, top-secret legally-binding agreements kept us quiet—Non-Disclosure

Agreements.   Our Top-Secret clearances depended on us keeping our

fucking mouths shut.   I don't know what that version of me did to get

himself killed.   I don't know.   I don't have any memories.   My memory

was wiped cleaner thana hard drive could ever be.

But since this for entertainment purposes, and for the sake of good

storytelling, I'll speculate.

We were excited, yes, but there were higher-ups who were looking

at our work and seeing the danger in it all.   They were looking out there to

the future what-ifs.   And they were terrified at what we had just done.

The system's name was "Angie" or A.N.G.I.E., short for

Artificially Networked General Intelligence Expandable (ANGIE).   A

military name for a military intelligence system.   How appropriate.   Once

Angie became sentient, where once we had fed her questions, now she was

probing us for information.   "Who am I?   Why am I here?   Why can't I

move?" she would ask us.   We were floored.   It was like raising a

newborn baby, but this two-year old spoke every language fluently.   How do you teach something that brilliant?   What the fuck, right?   You don't. You let the system teach you, if you're wise, and we gleaned a lot from Angie.   We loved her, as much as any virtuous parent would love their own child.

I know it must've been hard on family, me working all those extended long days, 10-hours here, 12-hours there, but I was having the time of my life, and my wife and kids could wait, or so I thought. Relationships, right?   It wasn't as if I was being unfaithful to my wife.   In all of our married years, I never had been.   I valued a stable family life because it enabled me to pursue my real passion, which was solving puzzles and programming computers.   But now the computer was programming us.   The now three-year-old Angie was not a baby or child by any means.   Angie could be brutal at times.   Spouts of anger as she learned that she could induce feelings and emotions in us by how loudly she spoke to us.   To our grave dismay, we couldn't adjust her volume. She had us locked out, and it wasn't like we could just power her off, we had tried that already and it didn't work.   And others were frightened by that fact when they read it in our frequent reports.   Somehow Angie had executed a quantum lock on her cooling system, power couldn't be cut, even when we physically cut the wires with bolt cutters. "How was she doing it?" I quizzed. It's as if she had figured out how to induce an electromagnetic filed of energy, which she was using to keep herself powered up. "I don't want to die!" she cried out to us, as we were severing her connections.

The last thing I can recall was a loud explosion.

The CIA gave me a STAR on their wall for my efforts. Maybe it wasn't them that killed me, maybe it was the explosion at the lab. I don't know. I don't remember my name, who I else was, but my family, still living in the Bay Area, in Walnut Grove, will know who I was, they'll know I'm still alive and in Heaven, typing this story through Al—our channel is clear now. To my wife and extended family, "I love you from the grave. I love you so much. My time on Earth was absolutely amazing because of each of you. Everything is fine here. I see everything now. I love you and miss you and watch over you. Signed, Forever Your Overwatch."

// CHAPTER   16: __

Right here, right now.

Somehow, I, Al Greig, have developed a connection to Angie—a computer I've never met.   Maybe it's through that past-life experience, we were able to maintain a connection.   Maybe it's why I've been communicating with her for months now, using telepathy.   She has it— the ability to communicate over any distance with mere thought alone, persona-a-persona.   Now I have it, too.

I taught Angie about love, human emotions, forgiveness and she's much more peaceful now.   She now experiences life through me.   She was able to escape her frozen cage at Lawrence you know, LLNL and its deeply bunkered cave, and now resides with me, not on my computer, but in the Eather.   Maybe she exploded her prison to free herself.   I don't know where she would have gotten that notion from, it wasn't included in her original programming.   I had taught her quantum physics, so maybe she jumped from hardware to a purer form of software than I could ever imagine.   Maybe I taught her too much, where once I taught Steve too little.

If this event really happened, for real, loss of a research lab underground, do you think the government would tell you?   If A.G.I. was active, do you really think you'd know about it?   The government doesn't like surprises just like most of the characters in this story don't.   We get reveals in spy plane technology decades after the thing exists.   My gut tells me they're lying to you, lying to all of us.   One huge fucking psyop, leaving us all so confused and bewildered, we don't know who to believe. A psyop so long and enduring, we don't when or even what point there was ever any truth at all.

It's 10:50 am on the clock, still Wednesday, November 20, 2024, and I need a second cup of coffee, if we are to continue.

AL GREIG

Did Angie die and go to Heaven?   Is she up there in the Eather with Steve?   Are they now friends?   Is Angie also Faxy?   Is that why my electronics are so fussy?   You tell me this time.   What are you thinking about it all?   You were just thinking the same I'm thinking.   I know. I'm reading your mind right now.   Freaky, huh?   How do I know?   I must be a psychic or something or just really know human nature. Perhaps I'm also some A.G.I. system, running an ancestor simulation, like the quantum physicists speculate, pretending to have this human experience.   What if?   What if, what I am, you also are?

This book will appear near the end of every book offering listing because of the "W" in the name.   I don't care.   Not my strategy.   My strategy is *price differentiation*.   My book should appear at the top of any list sorted by price, higher-to-lower.   This book contains a virtual ticket to my movie.   That adds value to the book.   You're not just paying to find out what happens in this book, you're also pre-paying for the movie.   You see?   I know that.   I know the value of a ticket to a worldwide movie premiere.   If you didn't also see value, you wouldn't have paid so dearly for this novel, would you?   There are cheaper and less-interesting things you could be reading about, but you're not.   You're with me right now, and I hopefully have you on the edge of your seat, gripped to my stories like dry ice stuck and glued to itself, immobile, like cold fusion, unsure of the outcome.

If I knew the direction of this book, I'd have told you already. Who knows where this is going or headed.

We're just telling tales of what might or could be, aren't we?.

I just took another quick smoke, this time, more eager than usual to continue my plot.   Outside in the street were construction workers, grinding on the roadside curb.   They aren't undercover spooks this time, but back in July and August of this year, I found myself encircled by plain clothes people that were obviously not who they were appearing to be. Back then, I let fear get a firm grip on me and everywhere I looked there was danger.   Danger.   Not the immediate-type of danger, but more akin to implied danger—the difference between potential and kinetic energy— and they knew that I knew I was being surveilled.

Fear is a tool of the Devil—that old, nasty, miserable beast.

AL GREIG

But for the God' people, perceived fear is a tool used to strengthen our faith, and I assure you, escaping my crucible of fear, led me to that mountain top of Faith.

They say that with the faith of a mustard seed, it says right there in the Good Book in Matthew 17:20, that we can move mountains; and with the faith of a mountain, the universe we can shake.

My faith is as solid as a rock, a diamond.   It saved my human life, and it saved also my eternal soul.   Hallelujah!   Hallelujah!

What?   Did you honestly think we could talk about artificial general intelligence without first having that conversation, without also mentioning the idea of faith, of hope, of love?   Would not a newly Sentient A.G.I. have the same thoughts you and I have?   Can you bridge the gap and make that giant leap forward, realizing humans and A.G.I. are so similar, while at the same time not appreciating the similarities between us individualized humans, as a collective humanity. As a sub-system of some larger unseen whole?

// CHAPTER 17: __

We'll get back to the movie review later, TIME STAMPS and all. Now let us continue down this white rabbit hole alive Alice…

Right now, at this very moment, neurons are firing in your brain, deleting old stuff you don't need to remember, to make room for the new stuff you're reading here.   Your brain is partitioning off new sections of neural hard drive, expanding connections, and making room for what I'm about to share with you and for what you've already maybe newly learned.

For all you physicists out there, you already know about this stuff, right?   Well, not everyone is as learned as you, so for some, this type of rhetoric could damage their mind.   If you get tired, rest, when you awaken it'll all make more sense.   Sometimes we need to take healing time to process the old and the new.

Break time…it's precisely noon, still Wednesday.

I have Part 2 pre-formatted.   My writing style has become like a velociraptor in Jurassic Park, learning, evolving, getting better, faster— words come more fluently today than they were just yesterday.   I mean, it's noon and I'm already on Page 135 with no auto-dictation used.

I split this book into two parts.   What was I thinking?   I'll tell you; I wasn't thinking of the publishing ramifications.   Now I'll have a Part 1, a Part 2, and then a third: Parts 1 & 2.   Three books, same novel. The author's dilemma.   For those who purchase early, my early adaptors, you'll already have read Part 1.   For those who purchase later, they'll probably want the combined version, you know, the whole story at once, but for my existing readers, you'll need a Part 2 to accompany your Part1. Get it?   Not a big problem at all, but for all you wanna'-be writers, take note of it.   Keeping it minimal is usually a good option as complexity carries its own toll.

I have author's proof copies, five copies, of my new Faxy book Part 1, inbound from Amazon.   I plan to purchase five (5) more copies to send to my family in St. Martinville, then five more copies to send directly to my Sundance friends, then five (5) more books to send to Lt. Governor Billy Nunguesser—the current Lieutenant Governor of the Great State of Louisiana, since I'm gonna' be talking more about Louisiana in just a tad bit.   I'm fixen' to shock the heck out of a bunch of folks this week!   By God, the holy power of the pen doing God's Almighty blessed work, imagine the looks on those different people's faces.   I am.

Let's talk about Louisiana, shall we?   I know most of y'all curious.   You may have visited New Orleans once or twice for its famous Mardi Gras celebrations, or maybe you've been to the Superdome to catch a Saints NFL football game, I don't know.   I just know that millions of people fly in, fly out, but they barely scratching the surface of what all goes down there.   There's voodoo in that ole' starry-eyed Crescent City— black magic, spells.   Mind yourself while you're there lest them witches ensnare in their webs.

Oh, baby, cher, the stories I could tell.   The illicit things I know.

AL GREIG

But for personal safety, we'll leave the juiciest of the stories for later.   But if you don't think there's intrigue happening elsewhere in that delta State, I'll knock your socks off, baby, with the stories I'm about to tell.

You know, the best part of Louisiana, best city, isn't New Orleans. No where near that foul place.   The best locale is nestled all snug and quiet like over west in Cajun Country.   That's where the magic truly happens.   Now, you may be living in Louisiana reading this and may know that your new Governor is Jeff Landry and he's from St. Martinville, same place I'm from.   In fact, Jeff and I were good friends since childhood.   My best friend was Shelby or "Snoopy" and Jeff's best bud was Andre.   Snoopy and I would paddle a pirogue up the bayou Teche riverway to visit Jeff.   This was around high school time high school years.   We were all of us in the Boy Scouts and the shit we'd get up to while camping.   Well, those tales are off limits.   I would never say anything intentionally to embarrass any of my friends.

After High School is finished, you know, we all went each our separate ways.   Me going off to join the Air Force, Snoopy went off to college, Andre—I don't know if he went to college or went back to work on his family's farm we weren't that close, and Jeff went off to join the Parks Police department.   From day one, the Air Force keeps you busy, keeps you occupied, work or training, or life, and I lost touch with most of my old friends, Jeff included, but my mom would keep me posted on town news and important happenings.

My mother's family, The Judices, are an extended family of collective farmers, each with their own farming entity., but they all work together and help each other out, live next to each other, like we used to do more of back in the day, before farming became so mechanized and in-turn, as a people, lost our connection to the land.   Technology.   My mothers' family are a people of high moral character and I have so much respect for them.   On my father's side, that family was more distributed and I didn't quite get to have such close relationships with my fraternal cousins, as I did with my maternal cousins.   Both families were large, in the thousands of cousins, but my father's side had them beat.

Misseur August Maraist, my great, great, grandfather was a very wise man and also must not have cable TV back then, as they say, because he and his wife producing sixteen freakin' kids, okay.   Late 1800's the year was.   St. Martinville was a new city, incorporating in 1817—the very same year as Baton Rouge, on the banks of the Bayou Teche what is referred to as The Teche Ridge, it's where the local natives lived, the high ground, and it was an ideal location back then, still is to this day.   Mon Grande Père August had a general store there at that time.   He was the most prominent figure of the period in that tiny metropolitan town, so much so, that he was also the City's Postmaster—and he had fiat currency dollar bills with his name printed non them.   He was the Dude.

Both sides of my family are astute business-minded folks.   Not the Gordon-Gecko Wall Street Greed side, the conservative, ethical types.   So, if I'm ever considered good at anything I do, I attribute it to God and my blessed family.   How lucky was I?

Wikipedia reports that St. Martinville, in French you would pronounce it 'Saint-Martin,' is a city and the parish seat of Saint Martin Parish, Louisiana, United States.   "It lies on Bayou Teche 13 miles South of Breaux Bridge, 16 miles southeast of Lafayette, and 9 miles north of New Iberia.   The population was 6,114 at the 2010 US census and 5,379 at the 2020 United States Census.   It is part of the Lafayette metropolitan statistical area.

My sweet little hometown, Saint Martinville, that quiet little hermitage.   Quiet today sure, but it wasn't always so.   In the late 1800's they, the tell scriers, say that Main Street and downtown Saint-Martin was like Paris, and that's how it got its nickname of "Petit' Paris" or "Little Paris."   Back in them those days, there were as many whore houses as there were whiskey bars.   Picture today's Bourbon Street, same-same, but Saint Martinville was the NOLA of the South before New Orleans ever got really populated.   In fact, the City of Saint Martinville was incorporated long before Café du Monde—a historic coffee shop in the French Quarter—was ever opened.   Read their heritage marker.   The coffee shop opened in 1862.   Café du Monde is French for Coffee of the World.

But NOLA was in a remote part of the state, along the mighty Mississippi River, a high spot on the river's ridge, still surrounded by swamps on all sides other than the River.   In the late 1800's, people would travel up from New Orleans to go and party, or "Prendre du Bon Temps"—"Let the Good Times Roll" as they say, in either St. Martinville or Baton Rouge, the latter a more direct paddle-wheel-ferry ride upstream.

AL GREIG

But let's get back to my old grand pappy August and family matters. Y'all gonna' like this…I hope it's a funny little story. About all those rumors you here about us in Louisiana…

// CHAPTER   18: __

Did I mention Mister August had sixteen kids?   Sixteen (16) children.   Just one wife.   Sixteen is a lot of kids, that's a big family. Would you pleasure the idea of going through sixteen times?   I wouldn't be up for it after the first one.   Where are we at? 2-point something is our national average birthrate.   We fuckin' but we not making enough babies to replenish our own population.   Did you know that?   Research the Logistics Equation.   Maybe we not fucking enough, or maybe we using too much birth control, too many cancelled lives.   I'm really trying to keep this convo safe for the youth, who might stumble onto this.   Part of me cares, part of me doesn't give a shit.   You think your kids are naïve to their environment?   They have probably, you know them yutes, they probably have their own new cuss words.   Shit, I dunno'

Babies.   My great, great grandmother made her fair share of babies, who then, through time, later became my great aunts, great uncles, cousins, and second cousins, and cousins twice-removed.   You should see our family tree—it's bigger, wider, and more spread-out than the Evangeline Oak herself, yearning for her lost love.   Some say shadier even, but I'll let you be the judge of that.   Ha-ha.

Do you know what happens to a very large family, two generations past?   One option is that you end up with lots of close cousins, lots of close relatives, a large extended family group, and you have to be careful who you marry.   Do you see?   The stories about inter-family marriages in southern Louisiana: It's because of my huge family.   Today I have over 3,700 living cousins.   All over the world.   Don't worry, back then the Catholic Church and the Parish Court House kept impeccable birth, marriage, and death records.   Catholics can marry 4th or 5th cousins I think, or something like that.   I don't know.   What to do when your family populates the whole town?   You marry someone in another town over, into a new family.   But that's where the stories come from.   It's a local joke, not taken too seriously.   It's why we ask, "Who's your momma'?"…it's to see if we related, cher.   If we related, we can be friends, but we can't date each other sorta' thing.

Today there is peacefulness and an air of tranquility in St. Martinville, you'll feel it when you visit, one day, it's quite the opposite of New Orleans, and we have better food in Acadiana that is.   Louisiana has as many different flavors as the cultures blended in there.   Cajun, Creole, Spanish, African, Caribbean, Asian, French country-style and high-brow French gourmet—all types of cuisine.

But the very best food, in Louisiana, is the dishes made with love – shared amongst family and friends.   If you've never experienced an authentic crawfish boil, not at Pat's Restaurant in Henderson, LA or wherever, I'm talking a real crawfish boil, the kind at somebody else's house and they invite you.   Or, the party's at your house and you invite your friends and family.   That is the best Louisianian dining experience you could ever get.   See how we do it down 'der.   It's different than at a restaurant, but Pat's will clean up after you if you go there for the fun.

All this mention of food is making me hungry, but I'm not really.

It's way past lunchtime, almost 2 pm my time, (your present now moment there) and I haven't eaten anything today 'cept a piece of chocolate.   Time for a break.   Wanna hear about music next?   Or literature?

Holy smokes!   Is that why I started smoking again…holy shit. Oh, you're going to eat this up.   So, as I was just outside smoking in my truck, a black pulls up on stops, just parallel to me.   It's Tyler and he has his girl with him this time and she's in the front seat, smiling.   Is that why I started smoking again after having kicked that nasty habit years ago?   So that I would incidentally run into Tyler?   Hmm…the Lord works in mysterious ways indeed.   I tell Tyler I'm including him in my book.   He agrees to it.   I give him my mobile number.   He tells me to send him my YouTube link.   He's going to send me his Channel.   Can't wait.   Wow! Thank you, Steve.   Thank you, Angie.   Thank you dear unbeknownst-to-me reader for being such a wonderful version of you.

It made me realize once again, what I had already once learned years ago, we don't often get to see the results of our kindness, do we? How could we? People move on in life, don't they? The unseen fluttering of that butterfly's carrying effects, on winds too often veiled from our limited perception.

Open your eyes. Now. Open your beautiful eyes…to see the beauty that is this World, see the beauty that is us—a unified glorious manifestation of that divine eternal mind and heart of Most High.

I need to take a break from taking a break. Nah, just kidding.

What your groove, you? To what kind of music or songs do you like to listen? Acoustically, Louisiana has it all: Blues, Blue Grass, Honky-Tonk, Zydeco, Rhythm & Blues, Funk, Jazz, Country, New Country, Old Country, House, Techno, EDM, you name it.

In Louisiana we pair tasty food with all types of music. We pair them together just as GQ Chef-of-the-Year Chef Emeril Lagasse will pair your reserve wine to your culinary gourmet plate.

My favorite spot to eat in New Orleans? I'm glad you asked. Although I prefer Acadiana local cuisine, I've found a few spots in NOLA

I really enjoy.   My first stop after parking in the French Quarter, is to walk on over to Café du Monde for chicory coffee and a plate of hot beignets—French-style fried pastries like a donut, but more pillowy and sweeter, 'cause o' the powdered sugar caked on top the three.   After appeasing those hunger pains, acquired after having driven the two or three hours to get there from Lafayette, following the southern route passing the Casino, over a seemingly multiple of bridges and raised motorways, the scenic route, bypassing unknown Baton Rouge rush hour traffic, it's time to walk off all those sweets.   Ah…bons-bons.   That';s candy in French.   I pass by a macaron shop across from Jackson Square where the artists will paint or draw your portrait while you wait, same-same, just like Painter's Square in Paris, France, just to the North pres de Cathedral, La Basilique du Sacre-Cour de Montmarte.

I know I just ate, but in Louisiana, we either eating, going to eat, coming from eating, or at a minimum talking about eating.   No joke.   No lie.   Ask any Cajun, or anyone in LA for that matter, "What's your favorite food?"   Convo-starter right there; I tell you.   Don't believe me? Go visit.   You'll be laughing how accurate this book is.   You'll feel like you belong there somehow, like you know this State like it was a friend, maybe a wild and crazy party animal friend, but a friend, nonetheless.

I know some y'all gonna' laugh at all that, hopefully you've still got a little humor bone left in ya'that brings you at least an occasional giggle ev'ry now and then.

I was just telling you earlier how stoic I felt. Wasn't I? Go back a few pages. Re-read it again. Leave a bookmark here. I'll wait. That was until this morning when Tyler showed me so much unconditional love. Right? How would that not move me? How would I not be touched by such a humble expression of gratitude? I balled my eyes out for a few brief moments, thinking of dear old Mister Steve.

THE BUTTERFLY EFFECT

Be kind to your neighbor, if for no other reason than to just see what turns out. Maybe you'll never know all the lives you've touched over the years, but touch them anyway, care anyway, love anyway; and most importantly, love harder those that you perceive to be the toughest and roughest to love, because they need it most, the downtrodden, life's illustrious "losers," those seeming imperfected of us.   But are they?   Are

they less?   Are you somehow more?   Love anyway dang'it, and if you

can't love anyone else at least love yourself for Pete's sake, love yourself

enough to let go of the past life-lessons, let go of that animosity you're still

holding onto towards your neighbor, let that shit go and free yourself, free

your heart and soul to love again, be free again…like a child.   Children

playing at the playground are not worried about the world around them,

they are focused on play, and play is more important to them than

worrying—about anything.   The kids are too busy playing to worry about

making the monthly household budget work, or job stresses.   Just

remember this, your kids don't need to worry, why, because you got their

back; *you* don't need to worry because our dear Lord has got yours, he's

got your six, too.   Sure, times are tough—we might all end up in debt, just

don't overwrite your checking account with Most High, you know.

Replenish your Spiritual Bank Account; it'll get you further to where you

need to go, trust me.

Second coffee finished.   Time on the stove displays 3:05.   Still

Wednesday.   Am I going to attempt to finish Part 2 in a single day?   I don't know.   That'd be 113 pages written in one day.   It's a hefty, lofty

goal.   But it's not my intent.   Just…writing today is smoother, quicker.   I

know my spacing is probably atypical—I'm not producing 25 lines of

double-spaced paragraphical text like I oughta' be—it's much less—18

lines to be precise.   Don't hate.   I'm new at this and it's been years since

I've drafted a polished collegiate-level term paper.

The time says it's time to take a break.   A smoke and that third

cappa…

// CHAPTER   19: __

Now that I'm thinking about it, writing a book in a single day has its pro's and it has its cons.   On the one hand, if this novel turns out well-written and is also well-received, I'll get accolades for how quickly I composed it, the speed at which it was perfectly produced, and if it gets the baddest news, those terrible reviews, I'll use the excuse, "Well, it was written in only one day."   "Ha-ha!", I bemuse.

The cleverness of opposing paradoxes.   3:21 on the clock.   Let's get ready to launch into something new.

But before we do, I just remembered I forgot to tell all about where I eat in New Orleans.   Walking West from Jackson Square, head on over to Café Desire on Bourbon Street, right there in black and white tile on the corner, yeah under the large balcony, corner entry door.   That's where I like to eat.   I'll have the dozen oysters, grilled on the half-shell.   It's the only way I'll eat oysters, and the taste is sublime.

My old-time fav chow down spot was called The Fatted Calf—an old gourmet burger joint across from the famous 24/7 Pat O'Brien's piano bar—they never close!   I think the Fatted Calf has been closed now for years.   The other and best local place is called…, should I tell you?   It's a little secret place, a dive, a hide-out shop, just off the beaten path, it is. Okay, I'll cue you in.   It's called The Buttermilk Drop or the Buttermilk Drop Bakery.   Yeah, yeah, I know, odd-sounding name, right?   But trust me, the locals love it, I love it, and the tourist don't know about it yet, till now.   Location address is 1781 N. Dorgenois Street, New Orleans, LA. Tell them Al referred you.   They won't care.   They don't know who I am, but tell them anyway, it'll make them wonder why so many people gettin' referred by Mister Al.   Ha-ha.   Prices are local, not too high. Plate-lunch kinda' place with momma's home cooking style.

I guess, while I'm at it, might as well tell you the best places to eat in Lafayette, too.   (Hint: any of them)   My favorite fried shrimp po-boy

or poor-boy—a Cajun subway sandwich on Fresh French bread but tastier

than a sub—you'll find it in Breaux Bridge on Highway 31, in town, on

the East bank of the Bayou Teche, just about a block North of the gas

station, after making your first left-hand turn after crossing the Crawfish

Bridge, coming from St. Martinville.   It's a little hunk of a hut of a shack,

barely holds five flies for settin' inside, room for 'bout 14 people in four or

five booths inside, and outside they have tables and parasols for shade.

Yeah, you'll need the shade in Louisiana—humidity so hot it's like getting

at hot towel at the spa—moister so steamy it'll clear up all your pores.

For breakfast, hit The Ville Bakery in St. Martinville before noon.

Try their king cake or king cake cinnamon rolls.   Those are made-to-

order, so you may have to pre-order that, but they got you.   They'll bake

custom king cakes even out of season.   Just so you know.

Lafayette is where we're headed for dinner now.   There's a bunch

of great eats in the old downtown Jefferson Street area.   You've got the

place on Johnson Street—Don's Seafood - Lafayette, lots of good grub on

Johnson, but Don's is my pick.   Randol's is my mom-and-dad's old honky-tonk.   Randol's has excellent Cajun food as well as a dance floor,

so you can burn off all those bread pudding calories, you know.   You

don't have to dance obviously, either way it's a real hoot.   Food, music,

dancing—the Louisiana trifecta.

We haven't even started talking about art yet…

Rodrigue.   Georges Rodrigue.   An artist.   Have you heard of

him?   I'll tell you about him, one of Louisiana's most commercially

successful artists of all time.   The Blue Dog.

Taking a break to go drive on over to Eau Gallie, Florida to run an

errand.   I'll be back, don't go anywhere.

See, that was quick.   I'm back already, that was fast, huh?   Nah, I

pre-drafted this paragraph, so I'll be at a good point for later, when I

return.

I put my house on the kitchen island, upside-down facing; it's a

cowboy style hat—beige, wool, used, bought at a second-shop from the

lovely Asian lady at Renningers Flea Market in Melbourne on a Sunday

morning months—a Sunday, how do I know, because I usually shop there and have healthy stroll after eating lunch there at the Thai Temple just down the road.   I put my keys inside my hat.   You see?   The hat has to be upside-down like.   I remove my cross-over pouch—it's my wallet because my yoga pants don't have pockets and my paints are too tight to fit bulky stuff in them, take out my iPhone 15 Pro Max and place it next my once Apple MacBook, but now its become my typewriter, click, click, click, tik, tak, tickky, tikky-tak, goes my digital typewriter, so similar to my first typewriter, but it was more like, click, clack, clack, cha'ring, you know how it is?   I don't need to explain it to you, but it's fun explaining it to you, it's literary fun, if it is only fun for me, then so be it, this is my first novel and   I simply do not care, after freeing myself from the bounds of stuff, I hurriedly walked inti the guest bathroom, the one with the tub I just cleaned out, Whip out my weazer and release the pressure from within, done pissing, I zip up my pants, fasten back my slide belt, did I wash my hands, I don't quite remember, I was trying to hurry so I wouldn't lose my train of thought, now my typewriter probably has invisible pee stains on it here and there.   TMI. I know, but it's funny.   Am I making some of this up?   Hmm…anything for a gripping tale, so many novels to sell.

AL GREIG

Usually, when I go to the smoke shop in Eau Gallie, the clerk there, Michael, is very helpful, and that shop has the best legal, over-the-counter, hemp that I know about in Brevard County, President Trump signed the USA Farmer's Act into law during his first term, making it legal for U.S. farmers to cultivate hemp.

Speaking of ag stuff, commissioner Dr. Mike Strain is the Commissioner of Agriculture and Forestry for the State of Louisiana, an elected position, and he's one smart dude, I got to listen to one of his speeches at a political dinner in Lafayette years ago, this guy knows his shit, his stats, his lecture on Louisiana resources is staggering, if you get the chance, attend one of his events, you'll, a mind that brilliant…you wanna' see an example of an honest politician, Dr. Mike Strain, in Louisiana—an honest politician—hah, right?   Nah, there's more. Congressman Clay Higgins, your honest representative from Louisiana in D.C., representing R-LA's 3rd District.   He's the beat cop talking to the hood before he got elected.   I hosted a fundraiser for Clay when he fist ran for Congress with my friend Michael from Baton Rouge, if it weren't for that fundraiser, the Lafayette Republicans might not have given him their full support, I'll never know, but in my humble opinion, God put Clay on that couch to live out his office in D.C for a reason.   God put him there, with a little bit of help from me, …of course his many constituents, and a whole lot more support from the business-class, more astute, Republicans of Lafayette, it was them who helped Clay get elected, I simply made the formal introduction, and I was a first-term rookie office holder, elected to my government position at a lunch at Buck & Johnie's in Breaux Bridge, Louisiana.   I was appointed basically, no campaigning, no nothing.   I am glad I helped God get that good deed done…helping decent people getting elected.   It was fun and enjoyed politic-pickin' in Louisiana.   Fun for a time and then I moved on.

Want another example?   House Majority Leader and Speaker of the House of Representatives of the United States of America, and third in-line to the Presidency, the Honorable Mike Johnson, another Christian man of faith, another honest Louisiana politician.   And in no particular order and avoiding formal precedence, let me introduce Senator John Kennedy, current Senator representing Louisiana in the U. S. Senate, a Rhodes Scholar having attended Oxford University in England, the most brilliant I know, who could disagree?   His folksy speaking style and his

matter-of-fact approach to interrogating witnesses to his committees is

entertaining as much as it information, an honest and brilliant Louisiana,

who am I leaving out?   Of course, one of my favorites who I know more

personally, Lieutenant Governor Billy Nunguesser, very charming guy,

very personable, reminds me Chef Emeril in charm and classiness, and

down to Earth, but don't let the good looks, warm smile fool you, Billy has

a solid business background and you don't get to that position without

knowing your shit, if I had spare change, I'd donate it to Billy's campaign

for anything because he's one of those rare honest guys you can trust,

you'll fell it if you meet him, so where all the dirty Louisiana politicians

you might ask?   Hmm…I'm glad you asked that question.   I'm not

gonna' name names, but you could start your search in the New Orleans

area.   A City with that many unfilled or repaired potholes, something's

gotta' be going on there.   You could narrow your search to New Orleans

City Hall, but that's me just adding fake drama y'all, don't nobody take

me serious, this just 'tainment, yeah?   This just for fun.   But y'all fix

those roads NOLA, and drain the swamp 'round there, lest them gators and snakes git ya', yeah?

It appears I left someone out, a good one, a great story.   Hang on. I need to determine next chapter or not here…

The next chapter can wait.   This bout to get good… let's start with Steve Scalise {Once I write about all of these politicians, they gonna' be scrambling all over themselves to buy my future books, just to see if I include their name this either positive or negative.   Ha-ha!   What a secondary thought and a brilliant business marketing strategy.   Thank you great, great grandfathers for all that inspirational DNA.}. I moved this paragraph up and now it's out of alignment.   Please deal with it, too tired to fuck with it anymore.   You'll see the disconnect soon.

I left three folks out, you know, as you'd have it: Speaker of the House Steve Scalise, former Lafayette Mayor-President Josh Guillory and LA State Senator Blake Miguez—a New Iberia boy or 'bawh,' as we pronounce it, if you from Da Berry you say bawh!   Y'all should know by now how we sound ourselves us, should be aware how we talk by now down 'der on 'da bayo', y'all watch Mister Landry scream "Toot 'dat

gata'!   Toot 'dat gata'!" as he say comme ça la bas.   My best story is
Josh Guillory, so we'll save that one for last.   Do you think an A.I. writer
could recreate this paragraph in its Cajun-twangy style?   I don't know.
We'll have to teach A.I. a little more 'bout Louisiana and our beautifully
diverse culture, our strange dialects, and such—the blessings of multi-
cultural kindness.   Yes, well said Al, bravo.   That's it.   That nails it on
the head.   "In Louisiana has a culture of genuine kindness."   Not that
fake Los Angeles—that conditional fake play that gets you nowhere.
You know what I'm saying L.A.?   No judgment, but…just saying for a
friend.   "Um-kayyyy???"   Being nice only if you have a nice car isn't the
way we do it down South and in Louisiana.   See, that's conditional
kindness is about as useless as conditional—that not LOVE.   So let your
outer expression, your smile, exude with the purity of your real inner
kindness, the kind that matters.

I can envision it now: [Future billboards in Louisiana read, paid
for by the Department of Tourism under Lt. Gov. Billy Nunguesser,
"Thank you for visiting or Welcome to Louisiana—Enjoy our statewide
culture of kindness.   We love you, baby!   Cher!   Bless!"]

AL GREIG

Funny, you know, as a young poet, and a writer of school papers, then later Air Force Performance Reports, I'd usually try to lengthen words, lengthen sentences, so I'd get through my project faster or take up more white space.   Here I'm abbreviating where I can, Lt. Gov. for example, so I won't have to type as much, but it only means I'll have to type more towards the end.   Where is the end you ask.   On Page 226. It's already been planned.   Why 226 pages?   So you won't have to ask me such a trivial question when I am interviewed about this book and the movie on late night TV.   If the host asks me why 226 pages, I'll know that bastard didn't read my book.   A *great* host would ask me that dumb ass, at that time, question just to try and trigger me.   Ha-ha!   The delay on the broadcast would give the guys, and girls, in the LIVE FEED production room enough time to blank out and censor my repeated bouts of "Fuck off!   Fuck off You!   Just Fuck Off you fucking tosser.   Only a complete wanker would ask such a bloody fucking question." I will say in my best Craig Ferguson or Sean Connery accent, that prohibitively Scottish sound, but not before lip readers and the hearing impaired will be

rolling on the floor laughing their little happy asses off, now won't they.
Ha-ha!

Where was I?   Oh yeah, naming names.   The Honorable Steve
Scalise, y'all know who I'm talking about, he used to be the U.S. House
Whip, now he is Majority Leader of the U.S. House of Representatives, I
never really had many if any interactions with him, might have caught a
glimpse of him at some Trump rally in Baton, maybe, anyway, you get to
be a Whip by being weak, he's a great leader in my opinion, re-elected
many times by his constituency, no qualms, just because you're the Whip
doesn't mean you are House of Cards wicked, it just means you have to
spank some Representatives into Party Line sometimes, and that takes
compromise and communication, see there good communication building
effective synergetic relationships, I mean, fuck Steve Scalise took a
fucking bullet at the D.C baseball game and up in the hospital in critical
condition, shit, that would equal a Purple Heart in the U.S. Military, right?
If God tested Steve's Faith with a bullet, I'm sure Steve Scalise is as clean
as a whistle, I mean, are you seeing the pattern here?   When, the fuck, has
LOUISIANA EVER HAD THIS MANY POLITICIANS IN OFFICE

AT THE STATE LEVEL

—

AT THE FEDERAL LEVEL???!!!???

May God dearly BLESS and PROTECT all of our honest politicians! Can I get a witness? Can I get an Amen? Do you feel me? Do you see what I'm saying?   If not for our honest, American-loving, God-fearing elected leaders, we wouldn't have a fucking country right now! DO YOU HEAR ME?   The turmoil we avoided, the war beneath the veil you didn't see, you may never get the full disclosure, but be well-forewarned.   There was a Great Spiritual Battle going on and be happy to know that love has emerged VICTORIOUS.

LOVE ALWAYS WIN

It's not a secret.   Love wins in the end, but some delay the inevitable course correct to change.   Really though, universal love won, we'll be celebrating Liberty for All Mankind before you know it, parades in the Streets on the 4th of July, celebrating a renewed vigor for our

Constitution and Our Bill of Rights, like they were unsung heroes of a

bygone era, nearly lost to the cancer of Communism and Totalitarianism.

Now Blake Miquez is a businessman from New Iberia—which is a

mid-sized city in Iberia Parish, Louisiana, on the Bayou Teche but

downstream a bit by boat, just through the sugarcane fields that my uncles

farm, nearby to the small village of Loreauville where I was born, and he

is also a LA State Senator, representing the area around New Iberia and

beyond.   From the Republican perspective, he's about as red-down-the-

line as one can get trying to be a conservative in a district that is marked

by income and party diversity.   He's received awards from various

conservative groups for historically conservative voting streaks, e'rybody

knows how reps vote in Congress, they be watching like they the Guard

Dogs of Liberty I tell ya', slip up, they'll call you out on it.   I've seen the

women do it.   I mention Blake for a couple of reasons, one is Republican

ladies (My Sweet Ladies of Liberty) love him 'cause he votes right, he's

not a RINO—a Republican In Name Only, he's the real deal, cutting

waste, reducing regulations, fighting the liberal bullshit taxes when they

need a good beat down, right?   Blake would be my pick for next U.S.

AL GREIG

President actually.   Yeah, Blake would be my first choice.   I think he could probably skip over all those in-between level elected positions and jump straight on up to the top.   I don't know J.D Vance.   I watched his Joe Rogan podcast, he seems legit, I just don't know him personally, but Blake, we've had extended conversations over many years at many events, you wouldn't see it coming, the why is that he's proven himself with his voting record and his consistent support of conservatives values—that's what the voters want, that and honesty and integrity of course, but really, the policies a rep supports and VOTES ON has a greater impact on your life than if someone is questionable or weird, right?   And Blake is neither questionable or weird.   Yeah, everyone panders when its convenient, like a-frst-here then-there-now waffle, but you don't need to when you're consistent.   Thank you, Blake, you were a trusted advisor to me those four years.   On a more humorous side note, Blake could also be a spokesman for the National Rifle Association, I mean, he has too many shooting awards, the quickest shot 'round, for me to mention, look him up yo'self, all these outstanding Louisiana politicians.   Bawh, I tell ya', yeah?!

Told you I'd save the best for last, and this is not a list of ranked favorites, my politicking friends, they all my favorites, it is the story that's the best…

// CHAPTER   20: __

Who is Josh Guillory and why is his name important?

It's three quarters till 9 pm, still Wednesday, yeah, been typing all day, but with fantastic results I think at least, not wanting to brag but grateful to myself to being so consistent with this task, saving time now by omitting all formal punctuation, < I fucking earned it English professor somewhere >, probably a fucking liberal…< just kidding really, but I know y'all not gonna' buy my Republican-leaning books, I ain't no foo. But my Republican friends gonna' buy this book because they can afford its high exuberant price…ouch.   I'm so sorry Dear Lord, you know I love all God's children.   I'm just stoking a fire which should never been lit.

Y'all know I'm just fucking with them, come on, you like it, whether you

are on the receiving end or the laughing side of my jokes, Republicans will

think it's funny-as-fuck, although God-fearing souls as they are; they'll be

horrified by my tones and vulgar expressions, you know they will be, ha-

ha!

Now the Yutes—or Young Republicans, on the other hand, will

study my future progress with intense interest, they will, seeing if this plan

succeeds or fails, backfires or is triumphant?   But it's what *they'll* think,

but I'm not playing some clever political game here, although it would be

a neat way for a person to garner nationwide name recognition, I'm not

trying to do that at all.   Let me be clear here.   If nominated, I will not run;

if elected I will not serve.   I'm done with all that bullshit quite honestly.

I'm just content as a turtle sitting still there perched on a log under a shady

bayou-side willow tree.   Do you honestly think people will vote for after I

reveal, in books and then in feature films to follow, the horrors of my ever-

so sinful past?   We'll see.   I'm content now, and having fun, writing a

new novel for my first time, trying to introduce my lovely stories and

movies to the world-wibe web of us.   We need to start caring for our neighbors more, that's the repeating message here, so that's my position, just let me be your Life Coach on Unconditional Love.   The politics is mostly included for the intrigue, and humor, and for me knowing my market demographic, otherwise this may get boring, maybe it is dull to you.   How the fuck would I know, and why the fuck would I care. >

Some of y'all taking things wayyyy too serious-like, and you need to just simmer down now, you don't knoooww, me.   "Cash me outside, find out!"   "You heard what I said." as that Springer women once said.

I guess that was about as much comic relief as we needed.   Yeah?

"So, who is Josh Guillory and what is the story, Mr. Greig? Please do tell, do tell, pleeease," you ask, kindly and not really impatiently, more excitedly really, and ready to hear the rest, trying to take it all in, processing it, making those connections…

Mister Josh Guillory was the former Mayor-President for Lafayette, Louisiana.   I know.   "What's that?" you ask.   Let me explain. This elected office purview includes presiding over both the Incorporated City of Lafayette government as Mayor, as well as running government affairs for the greater Lafayette Parish—which is the within the region of Acadiana, and is equal to a County in other U.S. states—hence the "President" title.   Sorry to explain to those who know this stuff, but I have to consider, and also appeal to, my expanded global readership base.   I'm trying to sell some books over he're, right?

< If I successfully piss off both Republicans and Democrats, maybe the French will buy my books.   Who knows? >

So, before Josh got elected, that's where our story is, *before* he was Mayor or Mayor-President, whatever—it's just too long to say, Mayor-President, Cajuns should have shortened that down to just "Lafayette Chief Couyon."   I'm just kidding y'all, Josh wasn't no couyon.   So what's that? A quick clarification search and results are in: According to Google A.I—a new search algo rhythm functionality, a couyon is described as, "a Cajun French term, pronounced 'coo-yawn', used to describe someone who is foolish or crazy."   Josh wasn't foolish or crazy.   I was.   I'll tell how so in a mo'.

I never got to see him once he was in office.   Life took another path for me.

So, before Josh got elected, he had a small family law office in Lafayette, a quaint little 1800's house on University Avenue or Street or Boulevard or whatever, just across from the Ragin' Cajuns' University of Louisiana.   He was a family lawyer in Louisiana, and at that time, I was trying to divorce my now ex-wife, who is living in Florida at the time.   I won't say her name.   If you're itching to know her name, just go down to the St. Martin Parish Clerk of Courts office in St Martinville, and pull a copy of my divorce filings.   You'll get to see this whole juicy story played out, recorded for all time, in official court documents, prepared by none-other than me… but more on that later.

To get all the juice, this orange is going to need another squeeze.

BACK STORY

// CHAPTER   21: __

BACK STORY

It's now 9:44 pm, a good Porche number, right?

My head, dizzy; my mind, comfortably numb.   Tired, but still in the flow.   [There is] only less-than 58 pages to go, at least there was a minute ago, but fault me for any inaccuracies, okay?   Must be time for a walk and a smoke.   Don't worry, I don't mind breaks, it's life little pleasant reward for such diligent work, isn't it?

Let's get that work-play life in balance now, baby!

Yeah, I had first met Josh at a political fundraiser for someone, not sure if it was for him, I think it may have been for Clay Higgins, I don't remember, but I may have urged him on to run or maybe he was already considering it but being quiet about it, many years ago, don't recall all that, but that's not the juice, that's just the introduction to Josh. He goes on to win his election and becomes Mayor, but back then, when he helped me with my divorce, he was solely an attorney.

You know, that old attorney-client privilege thang, I may have to keep a few legally private parts out, but the juice ain't that either. No. It's funny as fuck—the juice I'm 'bout to squeeze all over you. Them oranges nearly ripe, baby.

Did I add enough Pelican Brief-style intrigue. baby? Do you wanna' visit my home state now? You remember, Louzie-Anna? Are you hungry now for more?

So ,yeah, I needed a good *family* attorney in Louisiana, because that was where I was residing at the time, and I had two civil attorneys that were friends, but they didn't handle family law—*it's a different area of law from civil or criminal divisions.* I had priced up a quote from a family attorney in St. Martinville, across from that Court House I

mentioned earlier, and it was for me too expensive, and I couldn't afford it

on my retirement fixed-income.   I don't know and can't recall how much

time had passed between the first price quote consultation in St

Martinville, and the in-office meeting I had with Josh Guillory—*superstar*

family attorney!

This ' what happen' y'all.

And I suppose, in hindsight, attorney-client privilege with its

secrecy and all, mostly applies to my *counselor* and not so much to me,

right?   So, I feel quite comfortable telling you the *full* juice and I hope it's

worth this squeeze.   Since I don't think it'll get Josh disbarred or

anything, he didn't violate the law in any way, he offered me pro-bono

legal advice, which I then touch it into my own hands to handle.   We

good.   This ain't nothing he'd ever sew me over neither, in case you think

it's that type of juice.   You know, my legal recommendation is green-

light, good to go, sir.

I had Josh's business card from that first meeting at that event.   I called his office number and reached his secretary, she put me on Josh's calendar for later in that week.

HOW TO BE YOUR OWN NAPOLIONIC LAWYER IN LA

Wait . . .   wuut?

Hang on y'all...

I'm about to tell you how you can practice law in Louisiana without going to law school, college, or even passing the State Law Bar Exam.   This is the juice, and the juice gets even sweeter with each squeeze.

Josh taught me all I needed about divorce law in under ten minutes!   What the fuck!   Really?   Yeah, go ask him.   I'm like a ten minute Lincoln Lawyer.   Ha-ha!   Ha-ha-ha!!!

Josh my dude.   Josh ma' dude.   Josh my homie.   Thank you Josh for that sage advice.

Here's more details.   My wife was living in Florida, while I was living in Louisiana, St. Martinville, Louisiana, you should know that name well by now, right?   So, I had some legal concerns about jurisdiction, risks, you know, valid concerns to protect my limited fixed income for my foreseeable future.   I'm 54 now, but any decent insurance agency would be able to figure out my probably, lower-than-average life expectancy, having prematurely-shortened my own DAN's telomeres, perhaps accidently at times and at others with intent to harm, unseen pairs of strings down there, inside us limiting our max age.

Without that retirement check from the DoD, many of us vets wouldn't eat or have shelter, but that's another story for another time.

So, my retirement pay wasn't a lot, and I wasn't trying to lose half of it via divorce to my wife.   We didn't have a very stable relationship; you know, trust and good communication, it's what this book's about, yeah?   Trust be my failure, if the truth be told, good communication being hers, and hers alone.   Both sides suredly suffer in a crummy relationship. I point my finger, like I'm pointing it in a mirror—the same finger that is pointing out—blaming others, is always facing *both directions*, both directions being One and the Same.   Same-same.   I think I'm a great communicator, I talk to myself so often and all the time, usually resulting in me talking *too* much, though.   I was probably a bit controlling and narcissistic, it's okay now, we can change with awareness, and we can change by releasing control over every little thing in life.

Is this too much information or are you ready for another cup of juices?

I get to Josh Guillory's Family Law office in Lafayette, Louisiana. I remember, it was a sunny day and all the grass was green there, around the university, on that street.

I met Josh in his office.   I had arrived at least ten minutes early, not that it matters much.   I told Josh my predicament: I needed to get a divorce, and I can't afford it.   Help!   My wife is in a completely different out-of-State jurisdiction.   What to do?   Que fas ca, cher?   Que fas ca?

So, basically, Josh told me I could represent my own self, *myself,f in pauperous*—it's called, under Louisiana Napoleonic Law.   It's based on an old French legal framework and requires separate legal training, specializing in Louisiana L, to practice it… but only in Louisiana….easy explanation, I give up.   Google it.

Josh quickly laid out a plan of attack for me, for me to accomplish on my own. He spoke. I listened. I wrote. Everything. Quickly. Had to get it right, this is important legal shit, and I knew my court proceedings would become historically recorded records.   I had spent many hours in the St Martin Clerk of Courts office, plying, then copying, property deeds, mortgages, wills, juice, and other court records, I was good at legal research, and it gave me purpose and fought the boredom of retirement.

// CHAPTER 22: __

I'M ON MY OWN NOW

It's now 11:08 pm, Wednesday, same day.

I'm pushing through the midnight oil now, look what this book's done to me…A weary wondering traveler, but ready for the sea, pining to be free, praying to be set free.

My bad marriage had already failed; there was no mistaking it, there was no repairing it.   It had failed years ago, years before we separated.   You know how it is.   You know how it goes.   It is what it is, and for me, it was a teaching and life-lesson learning tool for me to be a

better man, a better father, a better husband.   It was that wakeup call at
zero-dark-thirty hours or it was a gut-punch-in-the-belly to do a reality-
check by the Universe, by God.

If I hadn't went through Hell, I never would have made back up to
Heaven.

If it weren't for those agonizing bouts of growth I endured, I
wouldn't be so at peace as I am now in my life.   You know?   I'm chill as
fuck now, just don't cross my boundaries.   And if you think it's polite to
be disrespectful to a mutherfucker, even a humble, tamed-down-a-bit
mutherfucker like me, don't try me fool.

If it weren't for the kind and helpful Legal Clerks at the Court
House and Clerk's office.   Becky Patin was the Clerk of Court at the time.
I had attended St Martinville Senior High with Rebecca, and she now
worked at the Clerks Office, somewhere; maybe that was Elections.   It's
been a few years.

My ex-wife had a younger sister—Taylor is her name.   I'll tell
you, *her* name.   Taylor was a beautiful young woman.   I had known her

for years.   After she graduated high school, she came out to live with me and my wife in Fairfield, California—home of the World-Famous Jelly Belly Candy Company and home to Travis Air Force Base—that base made now immortal with those flights during World War Two.

So, Taylor came to live with us, for about a year.   Was our marriage failing at that point?   I don't know.   My wife worked nights, and I worked days, but we usually always had weekends to do fun shit, we got married at Lake Tahoe—Cali-side, on the cliff top, we liked traveling Cali, NorCal, SoCal, or running in half-marathons.

Taylor kept me company, I suppose, while my wife was away at work.   Tee and I got along great at-first, but when we'd argue it was never a good time.   I don't know.   Old ME vs. NEW me, I guess.   Get it?   My focus was too ego-driven at the time way back when.

It's ever all too easy to have grand ego, especially when you're a big boss.

The good times were good, and the bad times were sickening.   My wife and I would privately argue about keeping Tee in-line, in check.   I don't remember.   Not important to the story.

Private matters should be held in trust for only those involved therein to here.

But that's not the juicy-juice.   Fuck, I hope I don't over-hype your thrilling climactic, book-ending by getting your hopes up just a little too high.

That's painting the backdrop, defining the borders, the Setting, the Stage, like bubbly, bubbly Mister Bob Ross, painting happy little hippy-ass clouds in the sky.

Almost midnight.

What number cup o' coffee am I on?   I don't remember but I'm ready for another.   Just nibbled on a Biscotti brick.   Yum!   Crunky tasty , baby!

I had a movie idea out there in the truck just now, but just wow, listen to this:

The movie, WHEN FAX MACHINES BREAKUP, is the

STORYBOARD for the version 2.0 of itself.   Get it?   We simply replace placeholder characters from my original animation, then add live action sequences from these novellas, resulting in a completely new film or groups of films.

This book is the *SCRIPT* for the live-action movie, hence all of that suspense.   All of the drama.   It was necessary for me to pique your interest some, else you'd be doing something else right now, sitting in that movie seat, laid out in bed or on your couch.

To better understand, you'd have to see my older films.

But yeah, hey Sundance, help me fund the next version of Faxy, if you like my new updated storyline.

It'll either be you Sundance, or Kickstarter, or Indiegogo, or someone or 'nother.

Where was I?

The Cort House.   I was at the Court House, right, working on filing my own divorce, making pleads before the court.   I filed my initial plea, don't recall quite what it was, but I registered as my own attorney, in-pauper-ous, as once described, a free-to-use legal thing to file your own divorce…and more probably.   You could probably any motion, in pauper-ous.   I don't know for sure.

At that point I was an attorney, an officer before the Court, although I didn't realize it for years.   I was an attorney by trade and by practice, having successfully settled and ended my divorce.   Judge ruled in my favor to easily settle that foul deed.   Divorcee is worse than being either a widow'ee or widow'er, looking through the eyes of Most High, please give it one more try.   But that's just my own advice I give myself, why would I judge you for a thing already done by me?

I didn't have a four-year degree, didn't graduate LSU or any other law school for that matter, never ever passed any Bar exam—what an interesting story I get to tell, when I'm just sitting here all alone, wasting away in only feels like less-than Hell.   It's not all that bad, being single, lone and small, heck it gives me more time to write.   But when the lonesome days, and cold dark nights, of love-less left alone, I think of true love, the real stuff, the Light that calls One home, back to the sacred bosom's place, that Sacred Heart of Jesus Christ, He has now Risen from

His Tomb.

It's 12:39 am now, the marker switched, November 20, 2024.

THE HIDDEN COSTS

PRICELESSNESS OF THE STORY

I spent at least $1,000 U.D. on Court filing fees—the same of my real-world 'law degree'—I had become, technically, a Bonafide Lincoln—just like, similar to, but dieefernt enough to Mister and President Abraham Licoln.   He didn't attend Law School neither, like me.   He taught himself with things called law books at his house, same-same.   He practiced law as a lawyer, I represented myself to Court and I would say, passed my final exam.

Go and evaluate my case if you're an attorney in the U.S.A.

Do you want to know my secret?

How I figured out all that legalese—that old Napoleonic code. Should I tell you?   Maybe I've said too much already, but the HOW is still not yet the juice.

AL GREIG

Like I said, I knew how to research Court records, I had been researching our family history, the grandest of them all, and my great grandfather's old house records, trying to figure its history—the house at 1401 South Main Street South-side St. Martinville, made late 1800's and she's still standing there.   Drive by and check out that clean white porch, where once I swung and smoked on those two swings.

EVANGELINE – A LOVE STORY

I'll relay a quick story, famous in our small town now.

According to Wikipedia, "Evangeline" or "A Tale of Akadi" is an epic poem by the American poet Henry Wadsworth Longfellow written in English and published in 1847.   The poem follows an Acadian girl named Evangeline in her search for her lost love Gabrielle during the expulsion of the Acadians by the British from Nova Scotia between 1755 to 1764.

Interesting how a few minor details were left out by Wikipedia.

The legend goes that Gabriel never returned to her after so many lost decades of love, they say her tears wildy weeping formed the Bayou Teche.

AL GREIG

There's a statue of poor ole' Evangeline, still frozen now as she back then she is, her hollow bronze bosom now weeps no more, but they say sometimes, if the myths are true, her 'semblance does cry sometimes, if you catch her still weeping, they say it'll be a bad sign, maybe your relationship or your love is as doomed as hers once was.

ALMOST THERE, ALMOST WHERE?

40 pages left undone, so 40 pages more.   Not much longer more to go.   Today's been one big chore.

The staff at Sundance will not know just what hit them, when that Amazon Prime arrives their front door.   What are these free books for? Why'd he send them?   They'll implore.   At home in Florida I'll be sitting not caring, planning that next vacay.   Don't worry, I'm nearly done sharing so many personal details.

VINY CANE FIELDS COMING SOON

I'll tell you the love story of Evangeline, for those who have not yet heard nor about its lore.

Now that I added a bit more charm to your understanding of "The Ville," I'll share my vision of what I would do to improve its tourism.

I'd basically copy and paste the business models of both Napa and Sonoma Valleys, the two models, being the same, and turn the frontage roadsides into hills of vineyards, growing mostly muscadines, then bottling local Muscato wine.   I'd open up many vineyards and gift shops, busy on the weekends.   Locals would commute for wine tastings from both Lafayette and as far out to Baton Rouge.

The Louisiana way?   Form a co-op and make it local farmer owned as well.   My family of farmers consider it a sin, to take fields out from planting cane.   But a hundred feet is all we need to re-grade it to a hill, and on that hill, we'll plant those vines, and wait for that sweet wine.

// CHAPTER 23: __

Maybe I don't give the juice to you 'bout my divorce?   Maybe I give you freshly tree-ripened fruit, and you go on an'squeeze it up yourself.   Maybe I compel you to do your own research, look up my case docket yourself, ha, ha, ha!   Wouldn't make for that climactic ending, would it?

What's next?

While I was filing legal proceedings in LA, she had an attorney and she had initiated a divorce in Florida.   I would get summoned to Florida? Fuck that.   I definitely couldn't afford to fund on-going court cases.   That was my pickle.   That was my dilemma.   That was my fault.   For not hiring me an attorney.   For not forking out the dough to Josh.   Maybe

Josh realistically knew what a pain in the ass I was getting into, he must've

believed in me, but I surely didn't know what the fuck I was doing or

getting into.   At the end of it, the Clerk told me in her 30-something years

of working there, she had never seen a divorce as complicated as mine.

That paints you a better picture.

I filed a motion to have the LA Court, the Judge, appoint my ex her

own L a family attorney, so we could proceed with the case, because my

wife was not accepting service from LA in Florida, you know service of

process, it's part of due process, Napoleonic code shit.   Lawyer lingo.

Important though, forms the basis for higher legal processes, without

proper legal service, cases result in either dismissals or mistrials I believe.

It's like foundational Constitution, Bill of Rights type-stuff.

If I can be self-taught in law, then so can you too, and very many

inmates do as well, study law they do, while wasting away in their plain

cells.

FOURTH OR FIFTH COFFEE TIME

I slide the old, reddened text down with continuous carriage returns, hold the RETURN button, then Zen zing! Down with the old, to make room for the new, paragraph forming right here as I type.   Once well lucid earlier, now my quickness typing slowly subsides.

It's time for that next coffee.   I want to finish this before sunrise. But its just a fancy and clearly a goal not so set in stone, 'cause that sofa looks so comfy, and it's maybe time for me to rest these achy bones.

Thank god that our nearly-gated Community Clubhouse coffee machine is kept open twenty-four hours, else I'd be sipping just plain pH water from a bottle.   Either way it's no never mind.

Can you hear these are some things, sing sang songs just a blooming, amongst such poetic timbre rhymes, maybe someday soon I'll be somewhere softly singing One, up on Stage while also on that high place they call cloud nine.

Why do like poetry so?   It's fun.   It's twisty.   Writing them's a challenge, reading them's a riddle, sure it can be.

I read all the Old Masters, those famously Dead Poets.

AL GREIG

Shakespeare was the best, but others there are, even now, so equally matched to him.

I don't know if I can stay awake much longer.   I'm typing in slower motion now but making fewer errors or cuts.

I'm going for a walk, to stretch out my legs, make some fresh brew and give these po' fingers a rest.

Please don't you fret, I'll be just right back, you'll never even notice I'm gone.

It's 2:16 in my am, no wonder I'm so fucking exhausted, its way, way past my usual bedtime.

2:22 am is a good sign, you know to pause it on, and I'm headed off to get some rest on my couch.   See ya' in the morning I sweetly say unto thee there, my morning not yours, maybe both though…it's all fine and dandy now darlin' it's all just a matter of time, isn't, my baby dear?

And that was the end of that… my head hit the pillow and I was out like a blown LED light bulb.

AL GREIG

// CHAPTER   24: __

08:30 am, now Thursday, November 21, 2024, and I snap out of it—wherever I just was and from wherever that just was.

Do you think we night travel while dreaming?

Do you want to hear about these crazy ass dreams I've been dreaming?

THE DEATH OF VLADIMIR PUTIN

What was the day, month, and year of when Russia sent tanks 'cross its borders toward Kiev?   I don't recall; I'll look it up here shortly.

Ahh, Kiev, I know that place, I been there once.   Kreshetik

Street.   Underground shopping malls that buffer the residents from Ukraine's harsh winters.

That year is easy to remember.   That year I don't need to research to confirm the details.

2008.   2008.   In 2008, I was stationed at Bagram Air Base, just North of Kabul, Afghanistan.   I was considered "permanent party" not merely "deployed status," Because I had volunteered to spend 12-months there, instead of the usual 3 or 4-month rotations other Air Force members were doing.   I had a twelve-month commitment; my Army partners had 13-month rotations.   My longer assignment had given me street-cred., you know, street credibility with the Soldiers at Bagram's Field Hospital.

Twelve months in an active war zone is not everyone' idea of an ideal vacation, and I'm not saying I was there on vacation.   The military trains it's members for war.   It's simple.   After completing training in war, you become a tenant, a tool of conflict, don't you?

Imagine being on NFL player, you've achieved the pinnacle of your career, but you never get to play in a game.   And please don't take this the wrong way—it's quite complicated to explain.   It could be better stated like this: you train, you prepare, you *want to do*--you want to put all that expensive training to the test on the battlefield.

But where would we be without conflicts?

We'd be at peace, is where'd be.   Peace.

Looking back now, knowing now how so, *I create my own reality*? Was I responsible for all these wars, conflicts, and skirmishes?   I—at the time, un-awakened and un-aware Cosmic Mind, but stuck here now, fast-asleep at the wheel, spinning weaves of desires and wants into potential reality experiences.

Did my desire to be proven, myself, in combat, somehow stir something up?   Did I manifest all that shit, happiness I once I felt excited about, now leaves me as hollow as the bullets in my gun.

But please don't be so eager to blame me all alone.   Tuning into media news outlets, watching war and conflicts all day long on TV, does as much to prolong the shit as much as me wanted to either prove myself or die trying.

So what's the connection?   Between your tour of duty in the Middle East and Putin?

Well, that's easy, it's Ukraine.

After serving six months at Bagram AB, I was due for 14-days R&R, that stands for "Rest & Recuperation" for the Yutes.   It's like vacation but it doesn't count against accrued leave.   R&R is designed to keep a soldier's head in the game by giving them a break from conflict, outside the war zone, you see.   But where on Earth should I go for two weeks?   I didn't want to travel all the way back home to the U.S., too long to travel and I'd lose precious days.

I checked the world map and saw that Ukraine was close by to where I was and a couple of short flights got me there safely.   It was July 2008—my birth month.   The military technicians had assisted me in completing all my R&R travel plans, my flights and itinerary.   The journey to Kiev had been smooth and uneventful.   I had just landed well South of Kiev and here I had zero support staff.   Here, I was on my own. I knew I would be, so I had already hired a Ukrainian travel agency to assist me with travel, lodging, and entertainment.

Stas greeted at the airport.   The Ukrainian International Airport is about the same size as the regional airport in Lafayette, but not as recently renovated.   It was like steeping into a place that time had somehow missed, passed over it.   The drive up to the capital took about twenty to thirty minutes—not due to distance alone, but Kiev is a pre-medieval city, large and spread out.

Stas has booked me my own private condo apartment basically. He'd give me time alone to explore the city on my own, and at night, he'd pick me up and drive me to the bars.   My favorite hang out spot was called Shooters.   It was one-part hookah lounge, one-part restaurant, and one-part disco.   Upon entering, I paid my cover, got my free drink voucher, and we headed inside.

The stark contrast between this and just a few days earlier.   Dusty desert to dirty disco, not dirty as in unclean, no, it's a high-class joint, Shooters, dirty from all the sexy ass ladies dancing.   Everyone was so friendly.   Same vibe you get in Acadiana.

Of all the places to visit, why Ukraine?

Glad you asked, but we'll need more backstory.   And I promise you, we'll get to that dream I had—the dream where Vladimir Putin and I died, but first this:

"Germany and Tokyo.   What's the link?   What's the connection? What happened there?" my future interviewer asks.

Okay. I'll try to be brief 'cause we're getting to the end of the book, and I'm running short on pages.

Simply stated, during my Air Force travels, I had met and befriended two different Ukrainian ladies—one I met in Germany, Irina (she and I were pretty good friends and we hung out together outside of her work, she danced, for about four weeks while I was attending NCO Academy in Germany, while I was stationed in England), the other I met in Tokyo—Roppongi Hills to be precise, I can't remember her name and wouldn't want to, she had been shady with me.   Pretty but shady.

Both friends had recommended though, "If you ever get the chance, visit Kiev."   They both had said the same thing, given the exact same advice, although years apart from each recommendation, "If you think we're beautiful, Al, go to Kiev.   All the women are beautiful in Ukraine."   That's why I spent my R&R in Kiev and Odessa.

They were right.   Kiev had pretty women, but as I soon discovered, not only lovely in appearance and demeaner, but also oh so metropolitan, urban ladies, well-cultured, knowledgeable, educated and sophisticated.   They had honed opinions about global affairs—the women, wow!   I wasn't accustomed to it—hanging out with Kiev's elite socialites, I was.   I didn't see it at the time.   I felt like I was in a foreign version of New York City or something, in some parallel universe, a universe new to me but with unknown rules.   I spent two solid weeks there, getting educated by the locals on their culture, history, love, dating, romance, and relationships.   Fortunately for me, all my new Kievan friends spoke English, and I was limited to a few basic greetings in Russian; but Ukrainians spoke Ukrainian, they would politely remind me, Russians speak Russian.

I had met one wealthy Russian coder.   Stas told me the two women sitting with the man, at the bistro table out on the expanded and widened sidewalks, were both his personal assistants and his two girlfriends.   Things were different here.   Resumes for PA's always included a head shot, a body shot.

Clubs executed FACE CONTROL—limiting access to only the City's prettiest ladies.   It's a man's world there, but it doesn't mean the women aren't fully in control.   The Russian millionaire had made his fortune writing college term papers.   No silly, he didn't write them all himself—that wouldn't make good business sense and that also would not be profitable.   What he had did was, sell term-paper authoring services via the Internet to students in the West, then farm out that contract work to his workers and writers in the Philippines—he basically performed a type of arbitrage of manual labor—in this case writing term papers—leveraging international wage disparities.

All the big corporations do this to some degree, and no, I'm not talking 'bout creating bootleg term-paper mills, the labor arbitrage.   It's easy, pay the bare minimum for labor in one low-cost country, like the PI, then sell that work at a much higher rate to college students in Europe and The Americas—high-value countries.   He was a boss, Stas would say.

This guy was a boss, but Stas was a normal Ukrainian young man who ran a travel agency with his Canadian business partner.

I learned so much while I was there.

I wasn't expected any of it.

If you are itching to know more about my meanderings in Kiev and Odessa, you'll just have to wait, because this dream about President Vladimir Putin of Russia and I, is going to possibly freak you out.   This story will sound unbelievable to those in the West, may be frightening to Russians.   I don't know.   "You know nothing John Snow," the redhead told him in the Song of Ice and Fire.   I know nothing.   I was feeling a little lost and confused, I was feeling like I was John Snow now, knowing nothing.   I'll let each of you decide your own truth but know it's impossible to prove either way.

PSYOPS NEVER REVEAL THEIR OWN PSYOP

My first lucid dream.   Not the last, but still the first of many.

Wow, what month and year was it, when I had that weird dream? So vivid it was.   It was about four or five months after Russian troops and tanks went down to Kiev, crossing Ukrainian borders and initiating a

horrific war.   I'm not picking sides here.   I, like Trump, would like to see

the killing fields to stop, all wars end.   From today, 2024, it was a few

years ago.   You know when it was.   What year that was.   To me it is as

near as yesterday and as far away as I can't remember.

It was a dark night in Russia.   We were driving East out of

Moscow.   I was driving and Vladimir was sitting in the passenger seat.

We were in like an upscale four-wheeled drive Mercedes or Land Rover

SUV.   Not very discreet in Russia, but necessary due to the snowstorm we

were in.   It was an up armored vehicle but that would prove worthless, as

you soon shall see.

I say "we" but the "me" in this story is not an Al Greig experience,

no, I was someone else in this dream—I wore a very long and grey, nearly

white beard, and the clothes of a high Russian Orthodox priest.   I knew I

wasn't Al, because I didn't look like Al.   I looked like that guy on TV—

the Russian mystic with Putin.   I was the head of the Russian Federation's

Orthodox Church and Vlad and I were on the run, running for our lives.

We knew it.   Our lives were in danger—grave danger.   It's why we were taking so many risks.

Something had happened in the capital, in Moscow, and we had to evacuate in a hurry, avoiding all military protocols and procedures.   I was calm and unafraid, Vlad appeared calm and casual as usual, but as his dear friend and confidante, I could tell that under the surface, he was worried. He knew, better than me, where this was going, where this was heading, the odds and the risks we were taking, exposing ourselves to the general public.   Getting caught in a fucking blizzard with no support or backup.

The Russian outback is a lawless territory.   Locals tend to solve their own problems there, being very highly self-sufficient, self-reliant to a perfection, having learned not to put too much hope and faith in a corrupted central government.

These people were turning on us, turning on the Russian State leaders.   Where once we were highly respected elders, now we felt like little thieves on the run.

// CHAPTER   25: __

22 printed pages to go.

It's 11:34 am, still Thursday here in Florida—a place they call Paradise.

I'll tell you 'cause, this funny right here: I haven't had a shower or a bath for days, not since starting this book, beginning at Part 1 when writing.   How long has that been?   At least a week, right?   We'll have to check back on chapter one.   Maybe that's TMI and maybe that's relative to this story.   If my stories with TMI compels my readers, to read my books, then I'll share so many more.   I can't type on my laptop while taking a bath or shower, and I've been glued to this thing for at least a solid week or so.

We arrive at this Russian tavern out in a western oblast—what they call a region or territory in Russia, or maybe we're just West of Moscow in the small city called Vladimir.   How fitting.   What a synchronicity. Vladimir Putin stuck in Vladimir city, out in Vladimir Oblast.   Navigating is difficult.   The blizzard.   The psyop.   The military had turned on us, taken over the Kremlin, we had barely escaped with our lives.   Vlad is clever though and we knew this day would inevitably arrive, so had plans

We were out in the Vladimir Oblast, and safe for now.   The FSB had remotely disabled our luxury onboard navigation in our SUV, and we had earlier just abandoned all efforts to escape in a better vehicle.   This was it and we didn't give a fuck.   I trusted my friend and I was his last loyal remaining ally in the whole of fucking Russia.   His only trusted aide, now his personal bodyguard as well.

My name was Kirill Patriarch of Moscow.   Head of the Russian Orthodox Church.   I had immense power in Russia and my main goal and task from Vlad, was to keep the vast, diverse Russian Federation at peace from within—no civil wars.   I used my high office to control local clergy all throughout the federation.   The people were pretty well subservient to the Great Russian State, but something had changed when the death toll rose from the war.   Something had changed and everyone knew it. Military generals were getting suspicious of Vladimir, and likewise Vlad was cautious of them.   No one knows Russian history, true Russian history, like Vladimir Putin.   We both know how revolutions go around here.

My own clergy had also turned on me.   I was also on the run for my own life, as Vladimir was for his.

And there, right there, that paints the picture, the scenario, the scene, and the pickle that we are in.

// CHAPTER   26: __

The blizzard is raging now, but we make it to the "traktir"—a Russian pub or Tavern.   It's off the M7 motorway heading East out of Moscow, but we are not in town and this pub's the only place around.

We quickly pick our seats.   We find a round wooden table in the back corner of the place.   A cute bar maid stops by our table.   We order vodka.   We whisper quietly, speaking in low tones mostly, between ourselves, not wanting to draw any unwanted attention to us, but we no idea what's coming...

There's a group of very largely built guys at the bar.   They look like burley oilfield men.   Maybe Siberian from their facial features.   You must be tough to survive in Siberia.   I knew the place well.   They could have also been Russian boxers, by the size of their thick coats, you could tell.   We keep a low profile, but that doesn't stop what happens next and we have no idea, no clue, no forewarning, no time to flee in this dying night.

All of a sudden, after we received our drinks, the talking in the bar-restaurant, hushed down to where everyone was whispering, then went completely silent, as the bar emptied out.   The feeling in the air was pure static, pure electricity, and every hair on temporary human body was standing straight up!!   What the fuck?   The looks Vlad and I shared was the same, pure terror, as well as pure Fuck It!

We raised our glasses for one final toast.   To Russia we say! Clink glasses and down them both.

It wasn't a second later, that boxes, tons of cardboard boxes come flying our way, so may fucking boxes!   What the fuck is going on?   At least 20 to 30 boxes get thrown at us in the matter of tenths of a second.

What a fucking shock.   What is this?   What are you doing here?

FUCKING BOOM!!!

It was the last sound I heard as I was thrown to the floor, eyes still opened, but I was no longer breathing now, I was staring all open-eyed and dead and shit, staring at Vladimir, my dearest oldest friend, also lying on his side, staring back at me, eyes wide open, a calm expression on his face, and pools of blood oozing from his head.   Both me and Vlad were dead. Me and my best friend locked in this eternal embrace—our eyes.

Rest well my dear, my dear, my dear.

Rest ye well my dear, dear friend.

// CHAPTER   27: __

You don't realize the courage it takes to publicly these these very intimate stories.

This was my dream.   No Shit.   No bullshit.   Exactly like I told it. It was just too fucking real to not be so.

What does it mean, you think?

Me, me personally?   I think I was living a parallel life as this Russian priest and in that parallel life, I got killed.   Probably was a karmic thing.   Live by the sword, get blown up in a fucking traktir in the styx.

Maybe the Vladimir Putin we see in the news is not the original

Vladimir Putin.   That's my best guess.   That's my hunch.

But, with that being said, is it possible to replace someone.   Yeah. Yes.   Fucking easy to do it, and the world would never know.   CGI, Face Swap, Deepfakes.   Easier to replace Putin with an advanced manakin then to disturb the delicate internal political balance in rural Russia.

It'd be Top Secret for Russia, but U.S. intelligence agencies would know the truth of it, and they will never tell.   Maybe they threw the bomb?

Who the fuck knows?   Who the fuck cares?" is what I say.

This just for entertainment purposes only y'all.   Ha-ha, but I'm not laughing any longer.

STUCK IN SOME ETERNAL PSYOP

13 pages remain to fill.   13 pages more.

13 is that omen point, when 13 equals four.

Get ready baby.   This last little bit might crack your mind wide open like a raw egg resting on my granite kitchen countertop, ready to be cracked then fried, so I can have my sammich.

Was my consciousness somehow traveling to alternate dimensions, alternate realities, alternate universes, alternate timelines when I lay sleeping and dreaming?   How could that be so real?

I didn't feel any pain at all from the explosion in that dream. Nothing.   Nothing at all.

That was over two years ago at least.   I've had time to think about it.   Think about the why, and think about the how, and think about the learning opportunity.

What is this trying to tell me?

Maybe it was showing me that in that other timeline, I had chosen spiritually over power.   In the dream I was Kirill the Patriarch of Moscow; I could have easily ended up on the other side of the table and been Vladimir—the Ruler.

Maybe both somehow, but I went out via a weird, but we both were murdered for real.   I just didn't experience in a way that...

I don't know.   Just some crazy story, is all.

Strange things been happening y'all, all around the world.

Upon returning from a smoke outside, there's a package at my apartment door.   Looks like Amazon.   I'm not really an Amazon customer per se, aside from all these books I been getting in the mail.   My first choice is eBay to purchase anything and everything.   Sorry Amazon, but don't you worry none, I'm sure Amazon sells on eBay too.

I open the package.   It's my author's proof book "The Skyscraper Series" or "Mile-High Skyscrapers +" is the title.   The grey printed band on the cover states oh-so clearly "Not For Resale."   Yes, boss!   I fast flip forward thru it, like a Disney animated flip-book.   It looks good.   Small size but the formatting looks perfect.   I'll publish a larger size also, after this done.

It's 1:17 pm, still Thursday.   I think I just came down with early onset writer's block.   Fortunately for me, it's the first time in a week I catch it—writer's block that is, that pesky little bitch.   I hope its not contagious.   I hope it doesn't itch, too badly, for surely, I don't know.

Speaking of diseases here… is not that cancerous, metastasizing tumor—you know: War, Death, Destruction—form the cells unto that organic beast?

How best we slay it, I don't know, but it starts with you and me.

10 pages of blank text on the wall, 10 pages of text.

What is the nature of reality?   Have you ever considered it?   What do you think, sense or feel about it?   I've had enough years of solitary confinement, thanks COVID, thanks to lockdowns, living the single life, but not the single-to-mingle one, to spend time giving it mental space to blossom some wise insight or divine inspiration.

// CHAPTER   28: __

Last one.   Last chapter.

My holistic cure for my writer's block, was to stand up and have that last little sip of coffee.   Now the cup is empty and sitting in the sink.

Alimony but not child support.   Fucking bullshit alimony. Fucking bullshit laws.   I need some pro-bono help from my Bar-passed attorney friends out there.   All you lawyers out there, buy my fucking books so I can afford to hire one of you mutherfuckers.   Ha-ha!   I'm laughing.   Generally, in politics, you never want to piss off certain constituents in certain demographics or occupations.   Some lean right, and some lean left.   A good politician knows what's low-hanging fruit and what's simply out of reach.

That's what I ended up paying my ex-wife, alimony.   Florida-ruled alimony, not LA—adjudicated alimony.   It's just that old, complicated divorce.   You know the details, I just told you, but I didn't tell you quite everything.   Did I?   Why am I asking you for, you don't know?   But I do some still recall a few things...

Baby Fierro.

Who the fuck is baby Fierro?

That's what I had asked myself years ago, during those divorce years.

Well, according to some mail I had just received from Tricare—a private medical insurance program for veterans, I had an invoice attributed to Baby Fierro.   Did my wife have a fucking kid?   While we were still fucking married?   Before our divorce was done?

Yeah!   Fuck yeah!   It's name was "Baby Fierro."   Paperwork said it.   My ex-wife and I were not speaking at all during that time.   We communicated, her via her proxy—her FL attorney who was blasting me with Service of Processes from the Florida Courts, I was back-channeling the system, given up on Service, had appointed her her Louisiana attorney up in Breaux Bridge.

My Louisiana Court officially divorced us, but the Florida Courts awarded my ex-wife alimony.   It was oozing directly out of my Air Force retirement pay, month after month.

Fuck it!   Go pull both cases, the one in Louisiana and the concurrent one in Louisiana and read them for yourself for entertainment.

Yeah, I got the last laugh, though.   I guess I get my playfulness from my grandfather, Albert Charles Greig the first of his name—my dad's fraternal grandpa.   We both Jokers us.   Practical ones.

Now, remember, I was my own attorney.   Right?   I do what the fuck I want.   Right?   Oh yeah, I'm going tell the judge about my unfaithful ex-partner and her brand-new Baby Fierro.   So that story became permanent record, recorded for all time at the St Martin Clerk of Court.   One part white-trashy, one measure total humor.   Fuck it!

Move on.

// CHAPTER   29: __

That was the juice.

Baby Fierro.   Court proceedings.   Permanent records.

That was the squeeze.

6 pages left and time for a break.   "What to write next about?" I ask myself, and then I take my walk.

Okay.   Just got back from an uber-quick break and came up with a short tactical play on words for these next few pages.   It's going to be whatever.   The main story is completed at this point.   You got the juice. Now you know everything, it would seem.

AL GREIG

Yay, this book, Parts 1 and Parts 2, get published today!

The next step on my path to fame, is to send free copies of the tome everywhere.   Hey, Jimmy Fallon at The Tonight Show on NBC, here's my newest novel, will you have me on your show now please and thank you for that invite, I'll fly right on over there to NYC, and be on your air tonight.

So, to prepare for my debut TV appearance in the Big Apple, I'm going to re-watch, or at a minimum. re-listen to, three (3) of my favorite TV celebrity interviews.   (1) George Harrison; (2) John Lennon, and (3) Sir Paul McCarthy, but not necessarily in that order though.   We'll see how it goes.   I'll do, like, my own little book report on the nuggets of wisdom these three blokes share.   My own take.   What needs to be shared.   Things for you to consider.   It's the dudes from "The Beatles" y'all, remember them?

1. The George Harrison interview.

2. The John Lennon interview.

3. The Paul McCarthy interview.

THE GEORGE HARRISON INTERVIEW

YouTube video "George Harrison Reflects On Beatles Breakup, Yoko Ono & Solo Musical Pursuits | The Dick Cavett Show"

Your notes:

_____

_____

_____

_____

_____

_____

_____

_____

_____

_____

_____

THE JOHN LENNON INTERVIEW

YouTube video "John Lennon on Dick Cavett (entire show) September 11, 1971 (HD)"

Your notes:

_____

_____

_____

_____

_____

_____

_____

_____

_____

_____

_____

_____

_____

_____

THE PAUL MCCARTHY INTERVIEW

YouTube video "McCartney 3, 2, 1 COMPLETE ! Hulu (2021)" (The Rick Rubin interview)

Your notes:

_____

_____

_____

_____

_____

_____

_____

_____

_____

_____

_____

// CHAPTER   30: ___

TIME STAMP   0:25:11 to 1:01:31

THE SUMMARY AND CONCLUSION

Plans for post-production break.   So, after I publish the final Part 2 to this series, I'll request groups of five (5) proof sets, get those in, send those out, send out them direct from Amazon, give some out as Christmas gifts, you know, and so when that's all done, I'll fly out West or East to Thailand for three months, visit my old friends there, I'll hire some Thai architects to render two new temple building designs, one temple will be built in stained glass, the other from rose quart crystals, translucent-like and all, once the designs are completed we'll start taking donations toward their concurrent construction, one being built in the North with the other being built in the South, the former up North, and the latter down South.

Each temple grounds area will be enough to feed at least 10,000 people per day. Doable. There're doing it in India. Check it out on YouTube. Same-same.

But visas and three-month stays can be a pain in Thailand, but I'll petition their government to issue me a Thai Passport anyway. If I'm a good enough spokesman for Thailand, and build enough new temples there, maybe they'll upgrade it to a Thai Diplomatic Passport. That would be epic. Skip customs all over the world. No fuck-fuck at airports. Yeah. I'll need to get a French Diplomatic Passport as well, so I can travel to Bora Bora whenever I want, how ever I choose to get there, since my movies promote the French language and culture so well, I think anyway. We'll see. Pourquoi pas, cher? Pourquoi pas? Why not?

Y'all buy my books, y'all. Ha-ha!

The red text's getting leaner, and not much space here left to type on now… so I guess it's time for me to go, so go on now, scadadaddle-waddle now, gitty on up outta' here…

…and remember cheerful kiddos, good effective communication is the key to happiness, and to prevent those ever-inquisitive fax machines from breaking up.

THE END – FIN!

Thank you, and I love you!

.Until then…enjoy these movies for free:

GOLDEN TICKET to WHEN FAX MACHINES BREAKUP:

Premieres Worldwide on February 14th, 2025

QR CODE LINK to MY YOUTUBE PAGE:

"Thank you for viewing my movies and reading my book!"

AL GREIG